Ludwig Bernstein

The Order of Words in Old Norse Prose

Ludwig Bernstein

The Order of Words in Old Norse Prose

ISBN/EAN: 9783337368821

Printed in Europe, USA, Canada, Australia, Japan

Cover: Foto ©Andreas Hilbeck / pixelio.de

More available books at **www.hansebooks.com**

THE ORDER OF WORDS IN OLD NORSE PROSE

WITH OCCASIONAL REFERENCES TO THE OTHER GERMANIC DIALECTS

BY

LUDWIG BERNSTEIN, A.M.

SUBMITTED IN PARTIAL FULFILMENT OF THE REQUIREMENTS FOR THE
DEGREE OF DOCTOR OF PHILOSOPHY
IN THE
FACULTY OF PHILOSOPHY, COLUMBIA UNIVERSITY

The Knickerbocker Press, New York

TABLE OF CONTENTS.

INTRODUCTION.

Of all the Teutonic dialects, only the *Anglo-Saxon* and the *Old Low German* have been examined thoroughly from the standpoint of word-order, the Anglo-Saxon in elaborate treatises by Kube,[1] Smith,[2] and Gorrell,[3] the Old Low German in an excellent dissertation by Ries.[4] Of the other great Germanic dialects, neither *Old High German* nor *Old Norse* is adequately represented, although Erdmann in his Otfried Syntax, as well as Holthausen and Kahle in their Icelandic grammars, could not help touching the subject slightly, while Mogk[5] has discussed briefly the *Scandinavian inversion* after the co-ordinate particle " ok." As regards the *Gothic*, I would say that an attempt on my part to investigate its order of words has led me to believe that, on account of its being almost a word-for-word translation, it is a dangerous thing to found upon it principles and theories. On the other hand, the occasional deviations of the Gothic from the Greek concern minor points and will be embodied in a separate paper.

It is hardly necessary to point out that the order of words of a language reveals its genius to no inconsiderable degree and thus constitutes an important chapter in its syntax. Due attention has been called to it by eminent scholars, not only in the line of Germanics, but also in Sanskrit, Greek, Latin, and the Romance languages. It is strange that the Slavic dialects, with the excep-

---

[1] Emil Kube : *Die Wortstellung in der Sachsenchronik*, Jena, 1886. Inferior in merit to :

[2] C. Alfonso Smith's lucid treatment of " The Order of Words in Anglo-Saxon Prose," in the *Publications of the Modern Language Association*, 1893.

[3] J. H. Gorrell : " Indirect Discourse in Anglo-Saxon," in the *Publications of the Modern Language Association*, 1895.

[4] John Ries : " Die Stellung von Subject und Predicatsverbum im Héliand," in *Quellen und Forschungen*, vol. xli.

[5] E. Mogk : " Die Inversion von Subject und Predicat in den Nordischen Sprachen," *Indogermanische Forschungen*, vol. iv.

tion perhaps of Russian in Gretsch's chapter on the order of words, have been so obstinately neglected even by so great a scholar as Miklosich, although the subject would be rich in interesting results. As regards a comparative treatment of the Germanic order of words, we still lack it sorely, and if the present paper on the Old Norse should be considered as a modest contribution to that question, I shall be amply rewarded for the time and energy I have spent upon it.

In taking up the question of the Old Norse order of words I have confined myself to the syntactic or grammatical aspect of the question—that is, to the prose, thus ignoring the poetic-rhetorical arrangement of words, and within the rich province of prose about 80 pages of the *Younger Edda* (Gylfaginning and Bragarœður [1]) were chosen, further about 100 pages of the *Olafssaga Tryggvasonar* [2] (chapters 59–84, and chapters 124–150), and finally over 50 pages of the *Eyrbyggja Saga* [3] (chapters 1–18, and chapters 41–57), altogether about 240 pages. This has been thought a sufficiently large amount of prose upon which to base a discussion of the order of words ; in fact, 100 pages might have done as well. Confining myself strictly to the immediate facts in Old Norse and making but occasional use of the other Teutonic dialects, I have ignored the pre-Germanic order of words entirely.

---

[1] Quoted simply as Gylf. Ernst Wilken's *Die Prosaische Edda*, Paderborn, 1877, has been used.

[2] *Fornmanna Sögur, Fyrsta Bindi*, Kaupmannahöfn, 1825. Quoted as Olafs.

[3] *Eyrbyggia Saga*, herausgegeben von G. Vigfusson, Leipzig, 1864, quoted as Eyrb.

ORDER OF WORDS IN OLD NORSE PROSE.

I. INDEPENDENT DECLARATIVE CLAUSES.

A. NORMAL ORDER.

(1) *Subject and Predicate.*

(a) *Subject and Predicate Verb.*

In accordance with the Germanic and Indo-European methods, the predominant mode of expressing the relation between agency and action, stripped of any modifiers, is in the simple affirmative clause : Subject + Predicate, which, for the sake of convenience, may be styled the "*Normal Order.*" Whether this is due to the principle of placing the more important, the Subject, before the less important, the Predicate (the so-called " Princip der Voranstellung des Wichtigen "),[1] is a matter of speculation which I dare not decide, especially in view of the fact that the Semitic norm for expressing the same relation is : Predicate + Subject, a fact which—if the above-mentioned principle be true—would naturally suggest that to the Semitic mode of thinking the action is more important than the agency. On the other hand, Abel Bergaigne[2] and Delbrück[3] advance the well-known ingenious theory of the Indo-European pre-historic order of words, which—to Ries[4] it is unquestionable—underwent the change into the Subject +

---

[1] *Quellen und Forschungen*, vol. xli., page 2.

[2] " Sur la construction grammaticale considérée dans son développement historique," etc., in the *Mémoires de la société de linguistique*, Paris, 1875, iii.

[3] " Die Altindische Wortfolge " (*Syntactische Forschungen* von Delbrück und Windisch, Band iii.

[4] *Quellen und Forschungen*, vol. xli., page 9.

Predicate order, also " vor der historischen Periode." The perplexing contrast between the two great families of the Aryans and
Semites is, of course, thus not accounted for, by any means, but it
is, after all, a question that belongs in the province of the Philosophy of Philology.

As far as the *Old Norse* is concerned, the normal order is, as sug-
gested : Subject + Predicate, as : Gylf. 5, 15 ; hann svarar : Gylf.
5, 16 ; Hár segir, and so in innumerable cases. In the *Gothic*
" Urkunde zu Neapel " and in the " Urkunde von Arezzo " we
find a sufficient number of illustrations to justify the statement
that the Gothic had the same order, as the formula "ik ufmelida "
indicates, which occurs 4 times in the document of Naples.   In
Old High German we find in Tatian for the Latin " sciebat enim,"
her uuesta.[1]   For the *Anglo-Saxon* Smith[2] claims the normal
order, and so does Ries[3] for the *Heliand.*

If 1 *Subject is put in relation to* 2 *actions*, the latter are in the
overwhelming majority of cases connected by conjunctions, such
as : " ok," " enn," " ne " : Olafs. 269, 7 : hann hljóp ok mælti ;
Gylf. 99, 9-10 : hann bauð enn mælti ; Olafs. 106, 13 : hann lék
né hló ; sometimes, however, the connecting particle is omitted,
as Gylf. 67, 15 : Utgarða-Loki fylgir, gengr.

3 *Predicates depending on* 1 *Subject* must be connected by
" ok," presenting in 23 out of 25 cases the scheme of Gylf. 11,
3, 4 : þeir tóku ok fluttu ok gerðu ; in 1 case " enn " is used instead of the second " ok " ; Gylf. 99, 7-8 : Baugi kallaði ok sagði
enn taldiz ; instead of " enn " " eða " is used once : Olafs. 273,
26 : sumir fellu ok brutu eða fengu ; not a single instance has
been found of the arrangement so frequent in German and English of : " er kam, sah und siegte," if the predicates are simple
verbs[4] ; nor is there any case in which the connecting particles
are entirely done away with.

If 4 *Predicates depend on* 1 *Subject* (there are 15 such cases) the
arrangement is free, although there is a tendency (6 cases) to
connect each predicate by " ok," as : Eyrb. 15, 25 : hón laut ok
tók ok brá ok lagði.   A very peculiar arrangement is Olafs. 113,
20 : við fórum ok bárum ok lögðum, gengum (4 cases) ; the ar-

---

[1] *Tatian, Lateinisch und Altdeutsch*, Sievers, Paderborn, 1872, page 319, line 1.
[2] *Public. Modern Lang. Association*, 1893, p. 216, etc.
[3] *Quellen und Forschungen*, vol. xli., pages 11, 12, etc.
[4] Compare, however, page 5.

rangement in 2 pairs also occurs 4 times, as : Eyrb. 96, 31, etc :
þeir tóku ok báru, gengu ok fóru, while in 1 instance only the
first 2 predicates are connected by "ok" : Olafs. 266, 2–3 : biskup skrýdist, ok vigði, gekk, hafði.

If 1 *action refers to 2 or more Subjects*, it is just as usual to place
the several subjects before the verb, as to place the verb between
the various subjects, as Gylf. 45, 8–9 : Guðr ok Rosta ok norn
ríða ; but Eyrb. 16, 1 : Eyjolfr hljóp upp ok hans menn ; if,
however, one of the subjects is a person already spoken of in a
previous sentence and, therefore, supposed to be well known to
the reader, the author employs the familiar construction of hint-
ing at such a subject by the demonstrative pronouns : " þeir, þær,
þau " placed immediately before the second subject, a construction comparatively rare in the *Younger Edda* and in the *Olafssaga*,
but frequent in the *Eyrbyggja Saga;* as : gerðu þeir Gylfi (that is
Gylfi and Oðinn) sæt sina.[1]   The " þeir," etc., in such cases may
also mean " the band, the folk, the host," of the following subject,
as þeir Þóroddr sátu þar (Þóroddr and his host), Eyrb. 100, 11.

In a combination of 2 *Subjects and 2 Predicates* the most frequent arrangement is that of : Olafs. 104, 21–22 : konungr ok
hans menn tóku ok vörðust ; another peculiar order is that of
Gylf. 10, 16 : hann fór ok kona ok helzt, so further in Gylf. 83,
11–12, etc. ; further noteworthy is the combination of Olafs. 153,
17–19 : raðgjafar ok höfðingjar lautu, sögðu : natural is, of
course, the occurrence of the following combination : Eyrb. 85, 1–
2 : þeir Steinþorr fóru ok drógu.   The result of our discussion
may be conveniently presented in the following table :

A. 1 *Subject and* 1 *Predicate verb.*

(1) Subject + predicate.

B. 1 *Subject and* 2 *Predicate verbs.*

(1) Subject + predicate + ok predicate (the majority).
(2) Subject + predicate + predicate (not very frequent).

C. 1 *Subject and* 3 *Predicate verbs.*

(1) Subject + predicate + ok predicate + ok predicate (23
cases).

---

[1] Poestion : *Einleitung in das Studium des Altnordischen*, § 169.

(2) Subject + predicate + ok predicate + enn predicate (1 case).

(3) Subject + predicate + ok predicate + eða predicate (1 case).

D. 1 *Subject and* 4 *Predicate verbs.*

(1) Subject + predicate + ok predicate + ok predicate + ok predicate (6 cases).

(2) Subject + predicate + ok predicate + ok predicate + predicate (4 cases).

(3) Subject + predicate + ok predicate + predicate + ok predicate (4 cases).

(4) Subject + predicate + ok predicate + predicate + predicate (1 case).

E. 2 *or more Subjects,* 1 *Predicate verb.*

(1) Subject + ok subject + predicate ⎫
(2) Subject + predicate + ok subject ⎬ equally frequent.

(3) þeir, (þær, þau) Subject + predicate (familiar and not infrequent).

F. 2 *or more Subjects,* 2 *or more Predicate verbs.*

(1) Subject + ok subject + predicate + ok predicate (majority).

(2) Subject + predicate + ok subject + ok predicate (less frequent)

(3) Subject + ok subject + predicate + predicate (rare).

(4) þeir, (þær, þau) Subject + predicate + ok predicate (rare).

(1) *Subject and Predicate.*

(b) *Subject + Auxiliary Verb + Predicate Noun or Adjective.*

Heyse regards as the "Grundform der deutschen Wortfolgelehre" the type : Subject + Copula + Predicativum, and reduces to it in a very interesting way all the phenomena of the normal order in German.[1] Convenient as it may be to apply it also to Old Norse, it does not seem advisable to do so, mainly for the reason that there are languages within the Indo-European group, not to speak of the Semitic dialects, which do not employ the copula ; for instance, the Modern Russian, in which the

---

[1] Heyse, Joh. Chr. Aug: *Deutsche Grammatik*, Hannover, 1886, p. 390.

auxiliary "to be" is practically not expressed in the present tense, but circumscribed—if an Adjective is the predicativum—by the so-called predicative ending of the adjective.

1 *Subject* and 1 *Predicate Noun* or *Adjective* are combined in Old Norse in the familiar way, the medium being the copula which regularly precedes the predicate nomen; the latter appears either as a substantive, as Gylf. 20,2 : þessi eru nöfn ; or as an adjective, as Gylf. 20,15 : hann er fullr ; or in the comparative degree : Gylf. 24, 16–17 : Ljósálfar eru fegri ; or in the superlative form, as Gylf. 31, 5 : hann er beztr. Very peculiar is the adjective use of "svá" followed by a genitive plural in Eyrb. 94, 3–4 : Kjartan var svá manna (such a man). As copulas are also treated the verbs : verða, þykkja, heita,[1] etc., as Gylf. 35,15 : Hestr heitr Gulltopr.

If 2 *Predicate Nouns* or *Adjectives* refer to 1 *Subject*, the coordinate particle is rarely omitted, as in Olafs. 288, 11–12 : hann var ríkr maðr, hermaðr mikill. In the majority of cases "ok" is the connecting particle, as Gylf. 14, 2 : hón var svört ok dökk ; sometimes "eða," as Gylf 33, 2–3 : hón heitir öndurguð eða öndurdís ; "ok þó" occurs in Eyrb. 14, 18–19 : Bergþórr var yngstr ok þó enn efniligsti ; "enn" in Eyrb. 11, 11–12 : hann var frændi en námagr .... finally "bæði ... ok" is found, as Olafs. 111, 27 : skógrinn var bæði þröngr ok myrkr.

If 3 *Predicate Nouns or Adjectives belong to* 1 *Subject*, the majority of cases shows a connection of only the last two nomina, as Olafs. 288, 12–13 : hann var ríkr maðr, hermaðr mikill ok újafnaðarmaðr ; so further Olafs. 259, 20 ; 300, 26–27, etc., Gylf. 10, 3, etc., a construction which hardly occurred, if the predicates were simple verbs ; the combination of Gylf. 31, 9–10 : hann er vitrastr ok fegrst-talaðr ok líknsamastr is rare.

If 4 *or more Predicate nouns or Adjectives* depend on 1 *Subject*, the treatment is free, although the arrangement in pairs appears comparatively more frequently, as Gylf. 40, 9–10 : fjöturinn varð slettr ok blautr, traustr ok sterkr ; sometimes out of four and even five predicate adjectives only the last two are connected : Olafs. 155, 7–8 : Sigvaldi var hárr, lángleitr, bjugnefjaðr, fölleitr ok eygðr vel. Occasionally only the first two predicate nomina are connected : Gylf. 37, 7–8 : Loki er fríðr ok fagr, illr, fjöll-

---

[1] *Cf.* Heyse, page 390, a.

breitinn ; further : Olafs. 155, 15–16 : hann var bæði mikill ok styrkr, fríðr, údæll. . . .

If 2 *Subjects* have 1 *Predicate Noun or Adjective* in common, there is only one arrangement, that of Eyrb. 21, 7–8 : þorsteinn ok Hallr vóru synir þeirra.

If 2 *Subjects* are connected with 2 *Predicate Nouns or Adjectives*, the arrangement is equally divided between that of Olafs. 287, 5–6 : einn var þorleifr, annar Ögmundr ; and that of Olafs. 267, 17–18 : bróþir hét Arngeirr ok annar þórðr ; or the "ok" is substituted by "enn," as Olafs. 255, 19–20 : sonr þeirra hét Ormr, enn annar þorvaldr.

All the combinations that fall under the heading of "Subject + Auxiliary + Predicate Noun or Adjective" may conveniently be summed up in the following table :

A. 1 *Subject*, 1 *Predicate Noun (or Adj.)*.

(1) Subject + copula + predicate substantive.
(2)   "   "   " adjective.
(3)   "   "   + svá followed by the genitive.

B. 1 *Subject*, 2 *Predicate Nouns (or Adj.)*.

(1) Subject + copula + predicate nomen + no conjunction predicate nomen (rare).

(2) Subject + copula + predicate nomen + ok predicate nomen (majority).

(3) Subject + copula + predicate nomen + eða predicate nomen (sometimes).

(4) Subject + copula + predicate nomen + ok þó predicate nomen (sometimes).

(5) Subject + copula + predicate nomen + enn predicate nomen (sometimes).

(6) Subject + copula + bæði predicate nomen + ok predicate nomen (sometimes).

C. 1 *Subject*, 3 *Predicate Nouns (or Adj.)*

(1) Subject + copula + predicate nomen + predicate nomen + ok predicate nomen (majority).

(2) Subject + copula + predicate nomen + ok predicate nomen + ok predicate nomen (rare).

D. 1 *Subject,* 4 *Predicate Nouns (or Adj.).*

(1) Subject + copula + predicate nomen + ok predicate nomen + predicate nomen + ok predicate nomen.

(2) Subject + copula + predicate nomen + predicate nomen + predicate nomen + ok predicate nomen.

(3) Subject + copula + predicate nomen + ok predicate nomen + predicate nomen + predicate nomen.

E. 2 *Subjects,* 1 *Predicate Noun (or Adj.).*

(1) Subject + ok subject + copula + predicate nomen.

F. 2 *Subjects,* 2 *Predicate Nouns (or Adj.).*

(1) Subject + copula + predicate nomen + subject + predicate nomen.

(2) Subject + copula + predicate nomen + ok subject + predicate nomen.

(3) Subject + copula + predicate nomen + enn subject + predicate nomen.

(1) *Subject and Predicate.*

(c) *Subject + compound predicate.*

If the predicate is a compound tense of the verb, the normal order is, " subject + auxiliary + verbal noun," the auxiliary thus occupying the position of the copula, the verbal noun that of the predicate noun of the above-treated type : subject + copula + predicate noun or adjective. Illustrations are : sá er nefndr, Olafs. 110, 28 ; further : hann skal standa, Gylf. 25, 12, or : þak hennar var lagt, Gylf. 4, 11 ; sometimes the auxiliary verb itself is a compound tense, and the dependent verbal noun is, differently from the German, usually placed at the end, or, better, after the compound form of the auxiliary, as : Hárekr lét gera kirkju, Olafs. 107, 24 ; but just one line after the author says ; Haroldr hafði látit gera (compare the Modern German : Har. hatte machen lassen), and with the dependent participle : nökkurir höfðu verit sendir, Olafs. 111, 19 ; on the other hand, there are also very few instances of the German treatment of that combination, as : Olafs. 149, 5 : hún hafði gipt verit = sie war anvermählt worden.

The position of the simple auxiliary after the verbal noun

hardly occurs in *Old Norse Prose*, is used very frequently, however, for rhetorical and rhythmical reasons in the *poetic language*,
so in the *Elder Edda*, Vafþrúðnismál 45, line 2 : þau leynaz munu
etc.   Smith finds it "in the *Orosius* most frequently in the so-
called progressive forms of the verb," in which cases "the auxiliary follows the verb proper, and thus occupies the extreme end-
position, thus exhibiting both marks of complete transposition "
(in the above-mentioned dissertation, p. 231).   Nor is the transposed order rare in the *Old High German* independent clause.[1]
In *Tatian*, page 69, § 11, we read : inti gefultê uurdun thô taga
sînes ambachtes," and in Latin : et factum est ut impleti sunt dies
officii ejus.   As to the *Heliand*, compare Ries, page 12 : ik fullón
skal, line 4767.   Here perhaps also belongs the peculiar extreme
end position of the verbs, although not of the auxiliary verb, in
the *Gothic* "Urkunde von Arezzo" (Stamm-Heyne's Ulfilas 230):
ik, Gudilaib, þo frabauhtaboka fram mis gavaurhta þus Alamoda
fidvor unkjane jah skilliggans .rlg. (133) andnam jah ufmelida.

In a *combination of 1 Subject and 2 Predicate compound verbs* the
auxiliary is generally employed but once, provided, of course, if
it is the same employed by the 2 verbs, as : ek skal styðja ok
styrkja, Olafs. 280, 14–15, and with the participle : dvergarnir
höfðu skipaz ok tekit. . . . Gylf. 18, 7 ; but for the sake of clearness the auxiliary is repeated before the second verbal noun, if a
clause or two or more phrases stand between the two verba in-
finita, as : konúngr lét taka hauk, er Astríðr átti, ok lét plokka. . . .
Olafs. 298, 22–23, and : sauðamaðr Snorra hafði verit á Öxna-
brekkum um daginn ok hafði sét. . . . Eyrb. 87, 4–5.

Instances of *3 Predicate compound verbs* being attached to *1 Subject* are very rare ; the auxiliary is in such cases employed only
once, and is placed before the first verbum infinitum, as : líkit
var sveipat enn saumat eigi um ok lagt, Eyrb. 96, 21–22.

If *1 Predicate compound* depends *on 2 Subjects*, the latter always
precede, there being no instance of one of the 2 subjects appearing after the predicate, as was the case with "2 Subjects +
simple verb predicate."   The illustrations are numerous : Sól ok
Bil eru taldar. . . . Gylf. 45, 2 ; 45, 10–11, etc.

A *combination of 2 Subjects* and *2 Predicate compound verbs* has
not been found.

---

[1] Becker, p. 436, § 285.

If a *Predicate Noun* is connected with a *Predicate compound*, we find in 22 cases out of 28 the predicate noun at the end, and the 6 cases of the predicate nouns being placed before the verbal noun occur exclusively in the *Gylfaginning*, as : sá maðr er nefndr Mundilfari, Gylf. 14, 16 ; but : sá er Surtr nefndr, Gylf. 7, 9.

Summing up all the possible modifications of the combinations : subject + predicate compound verb, we get the following table :

A. 1 Subject, 1 Predicate compound verb.

(1) Subject + auxiliary + infinitive ⎫
(2) Subject + auxiliary + participle ⎬ the only possible order.

(3) Subject + auxiliary + auxiliary participle + verb infinitive (most frequent).

(4) Subject + auxiliary + auxiliary participle + verb participle (most frequent).

(5) Subject + auxiliary + verb participle + auxiliary participle (very rare).

B. 1 Subject, 2 Predicate compounds.

(1) Subject + α auxiliary + α infinitive + ok β infinitive (regular).

(2) Subject + α auxiliary + α participle + ok β participle (regular).

(3) Subject + α auxiliary + α infinitive + ok α auxiliary + β infinitive (for the sake of clearness).

(4) Subject + α auxiliary + α participle + ok α auxiliary + ok β participle (for the sake of clearness).

(5) Subject + α auxiliary + α infinitive + ok β auxiliary + β infinitive (naturally).

(6) Subject + α auxiliary + α participle + ok β auxiliary + β participle (naturally).

C. 1 Subject, 3 Predicate compound verbs.

(1) Subject + auxiliary + α infinitive + ok β infinitive + ok γ infinitive.

(2) Subject + auxiliary + α participle + ok β participle + ok γ participle.

D. 2 Subjects, 1 Predicate compound verb.

(1) Subject + ok subject + auxiliary + infinitive.
(2) Subject + ok subject + auxiliary + participle.

E. Subject + Predicate compound verb + Predicate Noun.

(1) Subject + auxiliary + participle + predicate substantive.

(2) Subject + auxiliary + participle + predicate adjective.

(3) Subject + auxiliary + predicate substantive + participle (only in Gylf.).

(4) Subject + auxiliary + predicate adjective + participle (only in Gylf.).

(5) Subject + auxiliary + predicate adjective + infinitive (only in Gylf.).

A. NORMAL ORDER.

(2) *Object.*

Ries, in discussing the position of the verb in regard to the other parts of the sentence, remarks : " Im Anschluss an Bergaigne scheint es mir absolut mehr keinem Zweifel zu unterliegen, dass die Stellung des Subjects an der Spitze, des Verbs am Ende des Satzes, aller übrigen Satzglieder in ihrer Mitte,—wie es als das allgemein indogermanische Wortstellungsschema zu betrachten ist, auch die Grundlage der germanischen Wortfolge gebildet hat." [1]   He finds that in 11 cases out of 296 the object follows immediately after the subject and thus precedes the predicate. Smith,[2] and so also Becker for *Old and Middle High German*,[3] points out that in *Anglo-Saxon* the pronominal dative and accusative are regularly placed before the predicate,[4] a phenomenon well known in *French* and extensively used in *Russian*, in which it is not restricted to the pronominal object.   It was mentioned above in connection with the transposed order that the *Gothic*, in the fragment of Arezzo, has also the predicate following the object : ik . . . gavaurhta . . . jah skillingans .rlg. adnam jah ufmelida." Becker says that *Old High German* " lässt auch zuweilen das— (Noun)—Object dem Predicate vorangehen," and quotes *Otfried* and for *Middle High German* the *Nibelungenlied.*[5] No matter whether one believes that the poetic order of words, or, better,

---

[1] Pages 88 and 91, *Quellen und Forschungen*, vol. xli.

[2] Pages 219 and 220 of his dissertation.

[3] Becker's *Deutsche Grammatik*, p. 462.

[4] Compare also Kube's dissertation, *Die Wortstellung in der Sachsenchronik*, page 15.

[5] Becker, *Deutsche Grammatik*, pages 460, 461.

the poetic order, in rare exceptional cases is able to throw true light upon the order of the language,—the quotations from the *Heliand* and *Otfried*, few as they are, are interesting, especially since the type : subject + object + predicate is also the order of the language of the *deaf and dumb*.[1] As regards the *Old Norse prose such order could not be discovered* in the 100 pages of the *Olafssaga* that were carefully studied for that purpose, while, on the other hand, the *Elder Edda* employs it occasionally for reasons of alliteration and rhythm. The only order possible in Old Norse prose is thus : *subject + predicate + object*, no matter whether the object be a pronoun or a noun. Illustrations follow :

(a) *Accusative, pronoun or noun :* Olafs. 102, 1 ek segi þat ; Olafs. 106, 12–13 : hann tók ríki. Olafs. 108, 21 etc.: þeir brendu Kölni ok allar borgir (2 accus.) ; Olafs. 145, 20 : hann kallaði sik Óla (2 accus.).

(b) *Dative, pronoun or noun :* Olafs. 135, 4–5. þangbrandr sagði honum ; Olafs. 112, 14 : hann unni Knúti ; Olafs. 104, 13–14 : Olafr hét þeim makligri ömbun (2 datives).

(c) *Genitive pronoun or noun :* Olafs. 114, 18 : þeir hefndu föður sins etc.

The combination of *Dative and Accusative* shows, at a ratio of 3 to 1, that the indirect object precedes the direct, as Olafs. 103, 17 : hann bauð borgarmönnum grið ; so further in *Olafssaga :* 118, 12–13 ; 145, 24–25 ; 147, 3 ; 264, 20 ; *Eyrbyggja :* 97, 15 etc. In *Anglo-Saxon* the same tendency prevails.[2] The Dative follows the Accusative, for instance, in Olafs. 129, 19–20 : Haroldr hafði sent orð Hákoni jarli, etc.

The *accusative personal pronoun precedes a genitive noun*, as : hann eggjaði þik hins versta verks,[3] or a *dative noun*, as Olafs. 264, 8–9 : þessi vandr svikari hefir afsett mik allri minni eign ; and the *pronominal dative object* precedes a *nominal genitive object*, as : viljum vér unna hanum tignar.[3] This marked tendency of the Old Norse pronominal object to precede a substantival object occurs—according to Becker—both in *Old and Middle High German :* " Unter den ergänzenden Objecten folgt immer der Sachcasus, als Object der Art, dem Personencasus als Object des Individuums."[4]

[1] Ries, page 2, footnote.

[2] Smith, *Publications of the Modern Language Association*, 1893, p. 218.

[3] Poestion, *Einl. in das Studium des Altnord.*, pp. 129, 130.

[4] Becker, *Deutsche Grammatik*, p. 464.

A. NORMAL ORDER.

(3) *Adverb.*

Just as the object never precedes its predicate in Old Norse prose so also are the *adverb* and the *adverbial combination* invariably bound to the end position in a combination of subject + simple verb. Constructions like the *Anglo-Saxon :* þa hvælhuntan fyrrast go,[1] are monstrous in *Old Norse.* Ries, on the other hand, quotes 20 instances which show a similar structure : it undar iro handun wohs 2869.[2] A few illustrations will do for the Old Norse : úlfrinn gapti ákafliga, Gylf. 42, 1–2 ; þeir hestar heita svá, Gylf. 15, 1 ; þriðja rót stendr á himni, Gylf. 21, 3 ; mörg dœmi finnaz til þess, Gylf. 52, 1.

Of *two or more adverbs* of the *same character*, the adverb more general in meaning precedes the one of a more vivid and detailed description : þat er niðr í inn níunda heim, Gylf. 6, 18 ; annar endi hornsins var út í hafi, Gylf. 68, 22 ; gengu þau þann dag allan til myrks, Gylf. 58, 8 ; enn opt um daga . . . Gylf. 78, 12 ; exceptions to that rule are rare : viðir losna or jröðu upp, Gylf. 82, 3, compare also Gylf. 62, 18 ; 41, 11–12 ; 97, 20.

If the modifiers of the verb are *adverbial factors of different character*, there is a slight preponderance of the order : adverb temporis + adverb loci[3] over that of local adverb first and temporal second ; the ratio is 55 to 45 : þórr veðr þá eptir miðri ánni, Gylf. 79, 20 ; hann hljóp þegar út í ána, Gylf. 79, 4 ; stjörnur hverfa þá af himni, Gylf. 82, 2. On the other hand we read Gylf. 57, 9 : þórr dvaldiz þar of nóttina, and Gylf. 78, 13 : . . . hann falz þá þar.

In combinations of *external adverbs*, that is Adverbs loci and temporis, with *qualitative adverbs* (causæ, modi, gradus etc.), the genius of the language permits the greatest freedom, there being no absolute norm : as "eigi er nú fróðliga spyrt," Gylf. 16, 6, but : ok liggja svá víkr í Leginum, Gylf. 3, 12, and so forth.[4]

As regards the *position of the negative*, which in *Gothic* almost invariably, and—according to March—in *Anglo-Saxon* regularly, precedes the predicate,[5] it is distinguished by a considerable in-

---

[1] *Cf.* March, *Anglo-Saxon Grammar*, p. 220.

[2] *Quellen und Forschungen*, p. 91.

[3] *Cf.* March, *Anglo-Saxon Grammar*, p. 220.

[4] *Cf.* Heyse, *Deutsche Grammatik*, p. 395.

[5] So also always in Russian.

clination toward the present German norm, although the tendency is no binding law and disappears to a large extent in the dependent clause, as will be discussed later on. Parallel forms of the *German* and *Old Norse* in the independent clause are as follows :

The negative follows the simple predicate and shows a " finalizing " tendency.

(a) *Simple predicate.*

German : du weisst es nicht and *Old Norse :* þu fannt eigi, Gylf. 68, 7, 69, 6, 73, 17.

German : damals wusstest du nicht and *Old Norse :* þat sáttu eigi, Gylf. 69, 1 : þá trúði hann þeim eigi, 34, 17 ; 40, 21 ; 56, 5 ; 90, 4.

German : warum weisst du nicht? and *Old Norse :* hví spyrr þú eigi? Gylf. 50, 14-15, 74, 11-12.

German : schreien Sie nicht ! and *Old Norse :* látit þér eigi, Gylf. 61, 8.

(b) *Compound predicate verb.*

The negative follows the auxiliary and stands as near as possible to the verbal noun :

German : ich werde es nicht wissen and *Old Norse :* þessi man mik ekki skaða, Olafs. 286, 7 ; Gylf. 95, 13 etc.

German : . . . auch hatte ich es nicht gewusst and *Old Norse :* ok er þjálfi eigi . . . kominn, Gylf. 63, 21 ; 75, 19 ; 83, 15 etc.

German : das kann ich nicht wissen and *Old Norse :* þeira má hann eigi missa, Gylf. 30, 16 ; etc.

German : wenn . . . so wirst du nicht wissen können and *Old Norse :* ef . . . þá muntu eigi hræða mega, Gylf. 40, 25, but different in Gylf. 29, 11.

German : hast du es nicht gewusst? and *Old Norse :* hvart hefir þórr ekki þess hefnt? Gylf. 70, 7-8.

If the predicate is modified by 1 *Object* and 1 *Adverb* or *adverbial combination*, Old Norse employs on the first 100 pages of the *Edda* out of 250 cases 180 times the order *Object + adverb*, and in 70 instances that of *Adverb + object*, the ratio thus being 3½ to 1. The other *old Germanic dialects* are considerably freer in that respect. It should be noticed that the object which precedes the adverb is not only pronominal, but also almost as frequently substantival. Illustrations of the former character are : drepa

mátti Freyr hann meö hendi sinni, Gylf. 47, 13 ; ok báru hann
til úlfsins, Gylf. 38, 20 ; svá drap hann sik or Dróma, Gylf. 39,
13, and so forth ; illustrations of the substantival object before
the adverb are : Gylf. 33, 9 : hón á þann bœ á himni, er Fólk-
vangr heitir.   This example is especially interesting.   We should
expect that the relative clause which refers to " bœ " and not to
"himni" should follow immediately after the "bœ."   Other illustrations are : Gylf. 44, 5, hón gætir dura í höllinni, 38, 2–3 ; etc.
A few examples will do to illustrate the secondary tendency of
adverb + object : Gylf. 30, 2 : hann á þar ríki ; 33, 4 : Njörör
gat síðan tvau börn ; 40, 5 : þá sá hann á sinum bœ mikil hús,
Gylf. 3, 1 : Gylfi réö þar löndum ; 4, 10 ; 11, 4 ; 11, 12 ; etc.
Out of the 70 cases of the type : verb + adverb + object there
are 26 in which the dative-object would be expressed by a genitive possessivus in many other languages, as : hrafnar tveir sitja
á öxlum hanum = hans, Gylf. 48, 16 ; . . . ok lagöi á bak sér,
Gylf. 59, 11 ; . . . ok bítr í sporö sér, 38, 4–5, etc.

The *adverb* which modifies an *adjective* generally precedes it, no
matter whether the latter is placed before or after the substantive :
svá margir ormar eru . . . Gylf. 23, 7 ; furöu illa barnaeign gat
Loki, Gylf. 42, 7 ; geysi mörg heiti . . . Gylf. 29, 1 ; . . . at
gera borg . . . svá trausta, Gylf. 52, 9 ; etc.; irregular is Gylf. 83,
5 ; ok er sú björt mjök ; . . . hann veröa mundu ágætan mjök,
Gylf. 39, 5, so also Gylf. 39, 5 ; 38, 13 ; 82, 20.

If an *adverb* modifies another *adverb*, it precedes it, as Gylf. 70,
11 : hann bjóz svá skyndiliga, etc., there being no case in 100 pages
of the *Edda* of a modifying adverb which follows the modified
one.

While the predicate simple, as was shown at some length above,
never in the *normal order* of its predicative combination admits a
modifier (Object or Adverb) before it, the question naturally
arises, whether the *compound predicate verb* also always throws its
modifier or modifiers to the end, or better, whether in such cases
the verbal noun is tied to the auxiliary, showing thus the type :
subject + auxiliary + predicate + modifiers.   Smith asserts that
in *Anglo-Saxon* the "final position of the second member is the
most common if the modifiers are few," and quotes inverted and
normal sentences to prove it.[1]   Becker remarks,[2] on the other

[1] Smith, *Order of Words*, p. 217.

[2] Becker's *Deutsche Grammatik*, p. 469.

hand, that not only in *Old High German*, but even with *Luther*
the construction of subject + auxiliary + predicate + modifiers
(Object) "ist noch sehr geläufig." Ries did not separate the compound tense from the simple predicate.[1] As regards *Old Norse*,
240 pages have been examined (normal order only as being the
safest criterion) with the following result. Out of the 156 cases
with an auxiliary and verbal noun there are 6 that have no verbal
modifiers at all, and are, thus, neutral : Olafs. 115, 28, 134, 11 ;
303, 16 ; Eyrb. 88, 20 ; Gylf. 25, 12 ; 99, 4 ; and in 26 the only
verbal modifier is a predicate noun (Olafs. 110, 28 ; 111, 12 ;
111, 17 ; 112, 17–18 ; 115, 15–16 ; 116, 1–2 ; 116, 2–3 ; 116, 10 ;
116, 29 ; 128, 9 ; 250, 20 ; 255, 7 ; 276, 6 ; 276, 27 ; 280, 6 ; 288,
18 ; Eyrb. 11, 7 ; 14, 10 ; 18, 1 ; Gylf. 14, 16 ; 35, 12 ; 69, 3 ;
75, 8 ; 92, 1) which in the overwhelming majority of cases, at a
ratio of 5 to 1, stands after the verbum infinitum, as has been said
before. We have thus only 124 valid cases left, 47 of which have
all the verb modifiers after the verbum infinitum. Of those 47
cases :

(1) An *adverb* has been found only once, in Gylf. 94, 18 : enn
þat var sét síðarst.

(2) *1 or more adverbial combinations* occur 22 times : nökkurir
höfðu verit sendir til Holdsetu, Olafs. 111, 19–20 ; so also Olafs.
119, 45 ; 122, 9–10 ; 122, 14–15 ; 253, 3 ; 266, 25 ; 293, 5–6 ;
295, 12 ; Eyrb. 10, 1 ; 84, 1 ; 84, 29 ; 86, 19–20 ; 87, 23 ; Gylf.
4, 11 ; 21, 11 ; 32, 4 ; 32, 10 ; 44, 6–7 ; 44, 9 ; 76, 14 ; 76, 17 ;
77, 1.

(3) An *adverb* + *adverbial combination* occurs twice, Olafs. 118,
22 : hinn hvíti haukrinn hefir flogit lángt á eyðimerk ; so also
Olafs. 112, 3–4.

(4) An *adverbial combination* + *adverb* once : Eyrb. 84, 23 ; íss
var lagðr á Hofstaðavág mjök, etc.

(5) An *object occurs* 10 times : Knútr konúngr lét stefna þíng,
Olafs. 112, 24, so further : 114, 22–23 ; 129, 20 ; 149, 9 ; 150, 2 ;
262, 21 ; 264, 8–9 ; 264, 20 ; 293, 3–4, Gylf. 32, 8.

(6) An *object* + *adverb* is found once in Gylf. 74, 15 : ek mun
vísa þér til.

(7) An *abverb* + *objects* also once : Olafs. 290, 27–28 : Rögnvaldr lét hirða vandliga bæði afhögg ok spónu.

---

[1] *Quellen und Forschungen*, pp. 91–93.

(8) An *object* + *adverbial combination* 9 times : hún hafði gipt verít einum jarli á Englandi, Olafs. 149, 5, so also : 155, 14 ; 270, 22 ; 277, 2 ; 291, 22 ; Eyrb. 9, 5–6 ; 97, 20–20 ; 104, 2 ; Gylf. 30, 12.

It has been noticed already that there is a peculiar lack of illustrations with one or two adverbs after the verbal noun. This accounts for the fact that out of the 77 cases that are left for consideration, 43 instances (over one half) are found in which the auxiliary is separated from the verbal noun by *1 or 2 adverbs.*

(1) *1 or 2 adverbs :*

(a) *Loci :* hér : Gylf. 62, 11–12 ; aptr : Olafs. 118, 25–26 ; þar : Gylf. 93, 3, Olafs. 119, 16 : Ólafr var þar kominn.

(b) *Temporis :* áðr : Olafs. 107, 24–25 ; síðan : Olafs. 114, 14 ; Eyrb. 6, 7 ; Gylf. 39, 13 ; þá : Olafs. 118, 11–12, 124, 15 ; Eyrb. 18, 31 ; 84, 2 ; Gylf. 12, 11 ; nú : Olafs. 126, 12 ; 130, 10 ; fyrst : Eyrb. 96, 4 ; Gylf. 14, 3 ; hón var fyrst gipt, etc.

(c) *Modi :* svá : Olafs. 123, 14, Gylf. 25, 8 ; ekki : Olafs. 124, 11 ; 127, 29 ; eigi : Olafs. 138, 4 ; 353, 12 ; 286, 4 ; Eyrb. 93, 5 ; Gylf. 95, 13 ; enn örninn mátti eigi stöðva sik.

(d) *Other adverbs :* sannliga : Olafs. 113, 11–12 ; jöfn : Eyrbyggja 89, 10 ; ýmist : Gylf. 27, 6 ; ok : Olafs. 136, 12 ; 295, 26 ; Gylf. 43, 10–11 ; enn : Gylf. 37, 3 ; 50, 9–10 ; þessar eru enn nefndar.

(e) *Prepositional adverbs :* frá : Eyrb. 89, 5 ; við : Gylf. 55, 13 : allmikil fjölkyngi mun við vera höfð.

(f) *2 adverbs :* eigi lengi : Olafs. 257, 20 ; hálfu síðr : 284, 21 ; svá dauða : 292, 12 ; nú hér 292, 20 ; þá ok : Eyrb: 21, 5 ; hvergi víðar : 95, 3 ; svá nær : Gylf. 68, 3–4 : þú hafðir svá nær haft oss, etc.

(2) An *object* separates the auxiliary from the verbal noun in 10 cases :

(a) *Genitive :* þess : Olafs. 118, 13–14 : Gormr konúngr hafði þess heitstrengt.

(b) *Dative :* þér : Gylf. 52, 6 ; því : Olafs. 296, 4 ; engum mat : Eyrb. 95, 4 ; mörgum mönnum : Olafs. 146, 7–8 : ok þú munt mörgum mönnum koma, etc.

(c) *Accusative :* engan greiða : Eyrb. 96, 29 ; þá ferð : Gylf. 54, 17 ; engi tíðindi : Olafs. 101, 26 ; þik : Olafs. 264, 21 ; and finally the two accusatives in Olafs. 105, 10–11 : enn hann hafði allar borgir ok héroþ lagt, etc.

(3) *Adverb + object* stand between auxiliary and verb twice: ok bæ: Eyrb. 12, 20; ok kirkju: Eyrb. 92, 15-16: þóroddr lét ok kirkju gjöra. . . .

(4) *Object and adverb* separate the auxiliary from the verb 6 times: mik eigi: Olafs. 286, 6-7; þat upp: 289, 7-8; þér kunnigt: 296, 22; hofi upp: Eyrb. 6, 24-25; sér fátt: Eyrb. 15, 18-19; þat vel: Gylf. 99, 19: enn Baugi lætr þat vel vera.

(5) An *adverbial combination* is used for the same purpose 4 times: lengi æfi: Olafs. 288, 9; á land: Olafs. 147, 20-21; enn annat sinn: Gylf. 69, 16; til þess: Eyrb. 14, 15-16; Steinþórr er til þess tekinn.

(6) An *adverbial combination + adverb* occurs once only: af öllum vel: Olafs. 288, 4-5: þetta ráð var af öllum vel rómat.

(7) *Adverbs + adverbial combination* is also found only once: þar opt fyrir dyrum: Gylf. 50, 13-14: allþröngt mun þar opt fyrir dyrum vera.

(8) An *object + adverbial combination* separates auxiliary from verb once: þér at Oddi: Eyrb. 18, 28-29; ekki gagn man þér at Oddi verða.

(9) *The predicate noun* separates the parts of the compound predicate 5 times (compare above):

   (a) As a *simple predicate noun* 3 times only in Gylf. 7, 9; 42, 5, and 74, 7: sá er mistilteinn kallaðr.

   (b) In *combination with an adverb* once in Gylf. 69, 3: þát eru nú fjörur kallaðar.

   (c) In *combination with an object* once in Gylf. 90, 1: ok hitt mun þér undarligt þykkja.

(10) *Object + object + Relative-Clause* (the finest illustration) is found once: Olafs. 126, 7-8: enn Danir hafa kvikfé sitt ok alt annat góds, þat er þeir eiga, flutt þángat etc.

(11) *Apposition + adverbial combination* is found once in Olafs. 152, 12: þau naut voru öll einn veg mörkut.

Here must also be mentioned 2 peculiar cases in which an adverbial phrase of time separates: (a) *the copula from the predicate noun:* Olafs. 107, 3-4: hann var 5 vetr konúngr; and (b) the *compound verb from the predicate adjective:* Olafs. 128, 9: veðrit hafði verit um daginn kyrt ok bjart.

The discussion here would, however, lose its value without a further examination as to how many of the instances in which the auxiliary is separated from the verbal noun by a modifier show complete final position of the verb. Out of the 77 cases which belong here, in 48 instances we find verbal modifiers not only before, but also after, the verbum infinitum, while 29 cases, that is, about 39 per cent., show the complete final position of the verbal noun, whereby the following modifiers are thrown between the two constituent parts of the compound predicate.

(a) *Object* 4 times.

   (1) *Accusative* in Olafs. 101, 26 ; 264, 21 : ek hefi þik dýrökat.

   (2) *Dative* in Olafs. 296, 4 ; þú munt því ráða.

   (3) *Genitive* in Olafs. 118, 13–14 : Gormr konúngr hafði þess heitstrengt.

(b) *Adverb* 10 times.

   (1) *Loci :* Olafs. 118, 25–26 ; 149, 16 : Ólafr var þar kominn.

   (2) *Temp :* Eyrb. 84, 2 : hann hafði þá beðit.

   (3) *Modi :* Olafs. 123, 14 ; Gylf. 25, 8 ; Eyrb. 93, 5 : enn þórgunna vildi eigi selja.

   (4) *Other adverbs and adverbially used prepositions :* Olafs. 136, 12 ; 295, 26 ; Eyrb. 89, 10 ; Gylf. 55, 13 ; allmikil fjölkyngi mun við vera höfð.

(c) *Adverb + adverb* 3 times : Olafs. 292, 12 ; 292, 20 ; 294, 4 : Rögnvaldr hafði svá um búit.

(d) *Object + adverb* 3 times : Olafs. 286, 6–7 ; 296, 22 ; Gylf. 99, 19 : Baugi lætr þat vel vera.

(e) *Adverbial combination* once : Eyrb. 14, 15–16 ; Steinþórr er til þess tekinn.

(f) *Adverb + adverbial combination :* Gylf. 50, 13–14 : allþröngt mun þar opt fyrir dyrum vera.

(g) *Adverbial combination + adverb :* Olafs. 288, 4 : þetta ráð var af öllum vel rómat.

(h) *Object + adverbial combination :* Eyrb. 18, 28–29 : ekki gagn man þér at Oddi verða.

(i) *Predicate noun* 3 times : Gylf. 7, 8 ; 42, 5–6 ; 74, 7 : sá er mistilteinn kallaðr.

(j) *Object + predicate noun :* Gylf. 90, 1 : ok hitt mun þér undarligt þykkja.

(k) *Apposition + adverbial combination :* Olafs. 152, 12 : þau naut vöru öll einn veg mörkut.

It thus seems that the Old Norse employs a very interesting compromise between the Modern English and Modern German, with a most decided sympathy for the latter order.

B. INVERSION PROPER.[1]

It has been emphasized more than once that there is no exception to the *Old Norse law,* according to which the verb which is modified is bound to precede its modifier (object and adverb), and it has also been remarked that *Old Saxon* and *Anglo-Saxon* had various—the latter even numerous—illustrations in which said law is broken. This is a point of the utmost importance for our immediate discussion. For, if it be true that the verb-modifier (object and adverb) *must follow* the verb which it modifies, thus showing the strictest possible *local and logical coherence* with it, will not that very modifier, if—for some reason to be discussed later—it is torn out of the normal order and placed at the beginning of the sentence, show the same strictness of logical and local coherence to the verb? The question cannot but be answered in the positive. And, again, which order could better typify said closeness than the type : Verb-modifier + verb + subject, which is the retro-perspective, as it were, of the normal order (subject + verb + verb-modifier), and which type, for lack of a better term, we may call Inversion proper. This argument—to my mind—also accounts for the not infrequent exceptions to the rule in *Old Saxon* and *Anglo-Saxon,* in which dialects, as has been remarked before, the verb-modifier is by no means always bound to follow the modified verb.[2] Ries regards "das *Princip der Ideenassociation*" as a minor element in the making up of the inverted order ; but, on the other hand, I do not believe that his arguments as to the "stilistisch-rhetorisch-syntactische Gründe"[3] are valid, since they only explain why the verb-modifier is torn out of its normal order, without accounting also for the main point, why—the verbal modifier being given in an initial position—the *predicate* should immediately follow, and not the *subject.* It would be monotonous, and therefore, from a rhetorical-syntactical standpoint (which in-

---

[1] Interrogative and imperative clauses show inversion in almost all of the Indo-European languages. The inversion in such cases is subject to common Indo-Germanic feeling and does not properly belong under this heading.

[2] *Cf.* also Ries, *Quellen und Forschungen,* vol. xli., pp. 46, 47, § 13.

[3] The same, § 5–9.

cludes Stilistics), blamable to say : he came home, he ate then,
he read afterwards ; so in order to make the style more vivid
we place the verbal modifiers of the second and third clauses at
the beginning, and say : he came home, then he ate, and afterwards he read.   The parataxis is thus closer.   But while this ex-
plains why the verbal modifiers are placed at the beginning, it
does, of course, not explain why we should say : he came home,
then ate he and afterwards read he.

The initial position of the verb-modifier, especially the *object*
and its *substitutes* (verbal nouns, object-clauses), is, finally, brought
about for the sake of emphasis and stress ; that the emphatic
position could not be that of subject + verb-modifier + verb has
been shown above, consequently the only emphatic place of
abverb and object had to be that of the beginning, as it is contained in type : *verb-modifier + verb + subject.*

Before taking up the *Old Norse* inversion in detail, a few words
about the *Teutonic* and other dialects will perhaps not be out of
place.   Inversion is a common Germanic feature, and all the different dialects partake of it.   Aside from *Old Norse*, which hardly
chronicles any exceptions in prose, *Old High German* is more
affected by it than either *Anglo-Saxon* or *Old Saxon*.   Ries found
in the *Heliand* material enough to write a separate chapter about
the exceptions under the heading of " *Irregulär-gerade Folge.*" [1]
But in the case of *Heliand*, instances brought about by rhythmical
and alliterative considerations have crept in, which the *Old Saxon
prose* would hardly furnish.   As to the *Anglo-Saxon* inversion,
Smith remarks [2] that "inversion is a means consistently employed," and Mätzner, speaking about *Modern English*, says [3] that
"it has preserved enduringly echoes of Germanic connections of
words," and quotes copious illustrations of inversion.   *Old High
German*, in its development through *Middle* to *Modern High
German*, presents a great many interesting facts that have—to
my knowledge—not been recorded as yet, in spite of *Becker's*
elaborate treatise on the German " Wortfolge," a chapter of 56
pages. [4]   *Gothic*, finally, is not a reliable source as to the word-
order.   Of the non-Germanic languages the *Romance* dialects

[1] *Quellen und Forschungen*, vol. xli., pp. 47–56.
[2] *Publications of the Modern Language Association*, 1893, p. 222.
[3] Mätzner's *English Grammar*, vol. iii., pp. 535.
[4] Becker's *Deutsche Grammatik*, pp. 423–478.

know it,[1] while the *Slavic* (especially *Modern Russian* and *Polish*) use inversion very frequently, perhaps as a result of the Western influence (German and Scandinavian).[2]

As regards the *Old Norse law of inversion* it may be thus briefly formulated : If at the beginning of the sentence there is a word or words, a phrase or phrases, a clause or clauses adverbial or objective in character, the predicate, of which these elements are locally and logically a part, follows immediately and in turn is followed by the subject. That does not mean that all the modifiers of a verb must necessarily stand at the beginning. On the contrary, if out of 3 or 4 modifiers only 1 is torn from its normal order, the other modifiers may retain, in spite of the inversion, the place to which they were entitled in the normal order, as :

Normal : þeir fóru eptir þat suðr með landi til Norðimbraland.

Inverted : (a) eptir þat fóru þeir suðr með landi til Norðimbraland ; or (b) suðr fóru þeir eptir þat með landi til Norðimbraland ; or (c) með landi fóru þeir eptir þat suðr til Norðimbraland ; or, finally (d) til Norðimbraland fóru þeir eptir þat suðr með landi.[3]

Where a co-ordinate conjunction precedes a modifier, the inversion is due not to the conjunction, but to the modifier : for instance, in a clause like : "and there were many hardships awaiting them," the inversion is, of course, not due to the "and," or due to the fact that the "and" is coupled with the adverb "there," but simply to the adverb "there," which has the immediate inverting power. That would appear as a matter of course in the English inversion, but in Old Norse the co-ordinate conjunctions themselves, as will be discussed later, require inversion to a considerably greater extent than the German "und," "doch," etc.

Inversion proper in Old Norse prose always and in all possible modifications of Subject and Predicate takes place :

(1) After *an Adverb, Adverbial Phrase* and *Adverbial Clause.*

(2) After *an Object, Logical Object and Noun Clause.*

---

[1] Dietz, *Romanische Grammatik*, vol. iii., p. 463, 3.

[2] To Professor Leo Wiener I am indebted for this suggestion. Compare also the comprehensive work : Buslayev, *Historical Grammar of the Russian Language*, who, on page 372, quotes illustrations. I shall make use of the Russian and Polish material which I have collected in a separate paper.

[3] But compare, on the other hand, a clause like, Olafs. 149, 1 : enn þar fór um landit þingboð nökkut + subst. clause, explaining the "þingboð."

(3) After *a Predicate Substantive, Adjective, Infinitive and Participle*.

(1) *After an Adverb, Adverbial Phrase, and Adverbial Clause.*
A. *Adverb.*

(1) *Local :* hér or enn hér (4),¹ Olafs. 281, 23 : hér eru nú saman komnir margir höfðingjar ; þar (43), Olafs. 125, 4 : þar tók hann kaupskip ; ok þar (1), Olafs. 117, 26 : ok þar höfðu Danir sigr ; enn þar (1), Olafs. 149, 1 : enn þar fór þingboð nökkut ; þaðan, or "ok" or "enn" þaðan (5), Olafs. 144, 9 : þaðan sigldi hann vestr ; enn eptir (1) as a prepositional adverb : Olafs. 296, 4 : enn eptir mun ek vera. Only in the poetic passages quoted in the *Younger Edda* from the *Elder Edda* are there exceptions to be found : as Grímn. 14 : enn þar Freyja ræðr, or Grímn. 15 : enn þar Forseti byggir, etc., etc.

(2) *Two or more local adverbs :* enn niðr ok norðr (1), Gylf. 77, 3 : enn niðr ok norðr liggr Helvegr. Ok þar útan um (1), Gylf. 12, 4 : ok þar útan um liggr inn djúpi sjár. Altogether 57 cases.

(3) *Temporal adverbs :* þá (212), Olafs. 107, 2, etc. ; nú or enn nú (219), Olafs. 130, 14 ; 280, 10, etc.; síþan or enn síþan (30), Olafs. 131, 11–12 ; 106, 7–8, etc.; síðazt (1), Olafs. 253, 28–29 ; ok þegar (1), Olafs. 269, 4–5 ; jafnan or ok jafnan (2), Olafs. 280, 17 ; 288, 25–26 ; enn héðan (1), Olafs. 286, 7–8 ; ok aldri (1), Olafs. 306, 14–15 ; snimma (1), Olafs. 288, 15–16 ; fyrr (1), Gylf. 7, 1 ; fyrst (1), Gylf. 7, 6 ; næst (1), Gylf. 9, 12 ; opt or "ok" opt (2), Gylf. 59, 9 ; enn meðan (1), Gylf. 80, 18 ; enn áðr (1), Gylf. 81, 7.

Again the only exceptions were to be found in poetry : Grímnism. 11 ; enn nú Skaði byggvir, etc.

(4) *Temporal + temporal :* þar næst (3), Gylf. 13, 5 ; eptir þá (1), Olafs. 109, 25–26.   Altogether 285 cases.

(5) *The negative :* eigi, ekki, ok eigi, ok ekki, enn eigi, enn ekki : Gylf. 74, 4 ; Olafs. 304, 28, etc.   35 cases.

(6) *Causal :* því, ok því, enn því (19), Olafs. 120, 19 ; Gylf. 49, 3 ; þaðan (1), Gylf. 16, 3.   20 cases.

(7) *Miscellaneous adverbs :* ok enn (1), Gylf. 36, 1 ; lítt (1), Olafs. 298, 17 ; allmiklu (1), Gylf. 78, 5 ; gjarna or enn

---

¹ The numbers in parentheses indicate how frequently the word occurs.

gjarna (3), Olafs. 284, 30 ; nær = almost (1), Gylf. 35, 9–10; alt = throughout (1), Gylf. 17, 18 ; allvel (1), Olafs. 301, 4 ; svá or ok svá (26), Gylf. 3, 13 ; skjótt (1), Gylf. 15, 10 ; undarliga (1), Gylf. 49, 7 ; ok jafnskjótt (1), Gylf. 54, 12 ; vel or ok vel (2), Gylf. 63, 17 ; illa (1), Olafs. 263, 1 ; áheyriligt (1), Olafs. 304, 27–28 ; sannliga (1), Olafs. 271, 23. Altogether 43 cases.

(8) *Several adverbs of different character :* litlu síðarr (3), Olafs. 151, 10 ; nökkuru síðarr (2), Olafs. 117, 24–25 ; enn litlu síðarr (1), Olafs. 109, 1–2 ; enn þegar eptir (1), Gylf. 84, 5 ; svá mikils (adverbial genitive) (1), Gylf. 42, 9 ; ok svá langt (1), Gylf. 69, 8–9 ; ok eigi síðr (1), Olafs. 262, 17 ; ok því síðr (1), Olafs. 269, 19. 11 cases. Altogether 451 illustrations.

B. *Adverbial phrase.*

(1) *Local :* ok í hánum miðjum, Gylf. 7, 2–3 ; enn í Ásgarði inum forna, Gylf. 6, 3 ; ok undir hvert horn, Gylf. 11, 13–14 ; ok með sjávarströndu, Gylf. 12, 5 ; í þeirri kirkju, Olafs. 272, 6 ; á Náströndum, Gylf. 88, 4–5 ; í þeim stað, Gylf. 31, 12 ; frá Scotlandi, Olafs. 143, 24–25, etc. On 150 pages[1] 31 cases were counted.

(2) *Temporal :* í þann tíma, Olafs. 119, 13–14 ; á einu sumri, Olafs. 255, 28 ; ok at skilnaði, Olafs. 299, 16–17 ; ok í enda veraldar, Gylf. 7, 11 ; enn at vetri, Gylf. 99, 14 ; enn í því bili, Gylf. 58, 24. Enn um kveldit, Gylf. 51, 12, etc. The temporal phrases are very frequent. On 150 pages 112 cases were counted.

(3) *Temporal phrase + temporal phrase :* a því sama sumri eptir alþingi, Olafs. 273, 16–17 ; eitt sumar á alþingi, Olafs. 269, 15 ; and finally Gylf. 57, 9–10 : enn í óttu fyrir dag stóð hann upp. 3 cases.

(4) *Causal (source* and *instrument)* : fyrir því, Olafs. 150, 10–11 ; fyrir þat, Olafs. 270, 7 ; af þessum mönnum, Gylf. 89, 14 ; af þessu, Gylf. 98, 15 ; þar af, Gylf. 13, 19 ; ok af hennar nafni, Gylf. 34, 3 ; ór Ýmis holdi, Gylf. 12, 11, and so on. Illustration : enn af atkvæði guðanna urðu þeir vitandi, Gylf. 18, 9. 47 cases.

---

[1] That has been regarded as sufficient to illustrate "Inversion proper." Younger Edda and Olafssaga.

(5) *Miscellaneous adverbial phrases :* enn til þeirar borgar, Gylf. 12, 7–8 ; ok þar til, Gylf. 17, 22 ; enn á moti þeim, Olafs. 108 ; 13–14 ; fyr öngan mun, Gylf. 9–4. Illustration : allramæst var hann tignaðr um Austrveg. Olafs. 275, 18– 19. Altogether 10 cases.

(6) *Several adverbial phrases of different character :* ok fyrsta sinn á skóginum, Gylf. 68, 5 ; and 148, 11 Olafs : enn því nærst meðr guþs lofi skírði hann Ólaf. Altogether 175 cases.

C. *Adverbial Clauses.*

(1) *Loci :* enn hvar sem hann átti þing bauð hann öllum mönnum at láta, Olafs. 119, 20.   1 instance.

(2) *Temporis :* here the cases are very numerous.   Gylf. 46, 11 : ok er hann kom heim, mælti hann ekki ; Gylf. 69, 17– 18 : enn er þórr heyrði þessa tölu, greip hann til hamarsins; Olafs. 115, 24–25 : þá er Gormr var roskinn fékk hann konu þeirar ; Olafs. 138, 16–17 : sem hann hafði þessa luti séð ok heyrt, ætlaði hann. . . . Gylf. 4, 10 : ok er hann kom inn í borgina, sá hann þar.   76 cases.   Here the two cases belong which are apparently exceptions : Gylf. 12, 15, and 68, 18.   The former reads in *Wilken's edition* of the *Younger Edda :* þá er þeir gengu með sævarströndu, Börs synir fundu tré.   Such an order is *monstrous* in *Old Norse prose*, and is diametrically opposed to the genius of the language.   It is a glaring mistake, and certainly no im- provement upon *Jonsson's* reading, p. 19, 16 : þá er þeir Börs synir gengu með sævar ströndu, fundu þeir tré, etc., which is natural and in accordance with the spirit of the language ; the page G. 68, in which the other exception occurs, is full of anacolutha, and that special instance is an anacoluthon itself : enn er þjálfi þreytti rás við þann er Hugi hét, þat var hugr minn.

(3) *Causal :* Olafs. 272, 2–4 : ok fyrir því at hann hélt helga trú, var hann kallaðr Máni enn kristni.   1 case

(4) *Final negative :* Olafs. 132, 8 : ef landsherrinn slægist í móti þeim (lest perhaps) flýðu þeir þá brott, etc.   1 case.

(5) *Conditional :* Olafs. 258, 4–5 : enn ef honum hlotnaðust herteknir menn, sendi hann þá aptr til feðra sinna.   1 case.

(6) *Temporal + temporal :* Olafs. 259, 9 ; 268, 25 ; 139, 16 ; and 147, 17 : enn er ábóti var búinn ok allir vóru skrýddir gekk ábóti til strandar, etc.   1 case.

(7) *Several adverbial clauses of different character :* (*a*) *temporal + local :* Olafs. 149, 21 : enn er hún kom þar er Ólafr stóð, leit hún á hann öllum megin. (*b*) *temporal + substantive clause :* Olafs. 122, 8 : þá er keisarinn spurði, at Hákon var í Danmerk ok ætlaði at berjast í móti honum, sendi hann jarla sína tvá ; and according to Jonsson's reading : Gylf. 71, 8–9, which Wilken, p. 93, 12, changes. (*c*) *temporal + modal :* Gylf. 78, 10 : þá er guðin váru orðin svá reið, sem ván var, hljóp hann á braut, etc. (*d*) *temporal + relative :* Olafs. 111, 23 and 152, 27 : ok er Haraldr kom með herinn, er Hákon jarl hafði til forráða, tók hann at herja. 6 cases. Altogether 87 cases.

D. *Adverb + adverbial phrase :* (*a*) *one adverb + one adverbial phrase :* síðan at kveldi, Gylf. 59, 12 ; ok litlu fyrir dagan, Gylf. 60, 17 ; enn opt um daga, Gylf. 78, 12 ; enn eptir um daginn, Gylf. 54, 8 ; upp á himin, Gylf. 22, 2–3 ; snimma um várit bjó hann skip sín.[1] (*b*) *several adverbs + one adverbial phrase :* enn fyrir innan á jörðunni gerðu þeir borg, Gylf. 12, 6. (*c*) one *adverbial phrase + one adverb :* enn at morni þá, Gylf. 77, 10 ; enn at miðri nótt þá, Gylf. 60, 6 ; á hans dögum ofarliga, Olafs. 117, 15 ; enn um várit eptir, Olafs. 121, 29 ; and so forth, 16 cases ; altogether 22 instances.

E. *Adverb + adverbial clause :* (*a*) *one adverb + one adverbial clause :* Gylf. 3, 9–10 ; enn þar sem landit hafðdi upp gengit, var þar eptir vatn ; so also Gylf. 89, 12 ; (*b*) *one adverbial clause + one adverb.* The Old Norse is very fond of using the particle "þá" as a sort of convenient and reinforcing resumé after any dependent clause, especially frequently after :

(1) *The temporal clause,* of which there are no less than 75 cases, as Gylf. 10, 13 : enn er hann fell, þá hljóp svá mikit blóð etc., 13, 9–10, 74, 20 ; 68, 6–7 ; 34, 1 ; 58, 5 etc.

It will be remembered that we had 76, or almost just as many cases of temporal clauses without a following "þá." Considerably less frequently—9 times only—the reinforcing adverb is used after :

(2) *The conditional clause :* Gylf. 22, 13 ; 40, 24–25 ; 50, 16 ; 55, 8, 9 ; 77, 14. Olafs. 149, 25–26, 262, 8, 281, 18 ; 297, 30 : ef þú, konúngr, vill leggja . . . þá mátt þú þat svá vel gera.

---

[1] Olafs. 124, 27.

(3) *After a causal clause* 4 times : Olafs. 149, 25–26 ; 151,
26–28 ; 169, 1–2 ; 265, 13 : enn þvíat hvárigir vildu öðrum
samneyta kristnir men, þá var þat ráð tekit ; once in Olafs.
137, 29, the "þá" is substituted by "því" : þvíat þú tignaðir
aldri . . . því man nafn þitt víðfrægjast.

(4) *After a concessive clause* "þá" follows twice, in Gylf., 27,
14 ; 17, 1 : enn svá sterk sem hón er, þá mun hón brotna.

(5) *After a local clause* "þá" follows once in Gylf. 33, 10 :
hvar sem hón ríðr, þá á hón hálfan val.   After the *modal-
comparative* "svá" follows once in Olafs. 272, 21–22 : . . .
svá sem hann var fjarlægr, svá vildi hann.

(*c*) *Several adverbial clauses of the same or of different character.*

Any combination of clauses is possible after which, in what may
be called the majority of cases, 41, þá + inversion follows.   If
compared with the cases under 7, *b*, we find 85 per cent. with a
following þá, Gylf. 40, 20–21 ; 46, 6–7 ; 54, 8–9 ; 54, 10–11 ; 63,
15–16 ; 66, 7–8 ; 96, 14–15 ; 38, 16 ; 54, 4.   Olafs. 10, 9 ; 126, 25 ;
255, 31 ; 260, 28 etc.   One illustration : Olafs. 284, 12–16 : með
því at ek hefi svá upphafvit (causal), at ek hefvir fullkommliga
stadt upp (consec.) . . . enn alt landsfólk er hér rétt trúat (causal)
. . . þá skal ek eigi síðr ástunda etc. . . .

F. *Adverbial phrase + adverbial clause:* in the majority of
cases both the phrase and the clause are temporal : Gylf.
39, 1–2 ; 67, 11 ; Olafs. 111, 24 ; 111, 25 ; 138, 27 ; 265,
5–6 ; 273, 22–23 ; 290, 9–11 ; 259, 28–29 ; 280, 3–4 ; 260,
17, and finally Gylf. 9, 16 : ok inn fyrsta dag, er hón
sleikti steina, kom . . . manns hár, 12 cases ; in the following 2 instances the clause is a *relative :* Olafs. 294, 9–10,
and 151, 6–7 : enn með fé því, er Ólafr konúngr gaf þáng-
brandi, keypti hann mey.

G. *Adverb + adverbial phrase + adverbial clause:* (*a*) *the
latter order plus inversion* occurs only once in Olafs. 267,
13–14 ; enn norðr í sveitum, er þeir fóru þar yfir, tóku trú
göfgir menn ; and (*b*) in Olafs. 133, 13–14 a variation of
that combination is found in a case of *adverbial phrase +
adverb + temporal clause :* ok hinn næsta vetr eptir, er þeir
Ottó keisari skilðu, sat Ólafr í ríki sínu á Vindlandi. (*c*) *Adverbial phrase + adverbial clause + adverb* is represented
by 10 instances : Gylf. 11, 7–8 ; 20, 13–14 ; 51, 7–8 ; 52,

15–16 ; 72, 15 ; 92, 6. Olafs. 286, 12–13, 283, 13 etc. and 146, 11 : enn til þess at þú efist eigi um þessi andsvör, þá máttu þat . . . hafa.

(2) *Inversion follows after an Object, Logical Object and Noun-Clause :*

A. *Object* which may be either :

(1) *An Accusative :* (a) *pronoun :* hann, Gylf. 15, 17 ; 21, 7 ; 31, 5 ; 75, 13–14 ; Olafs. 250, 22 ; 298, 7–8 ; hit, Olafs. 299, 14 ; hana, Gylf. 16, 8 ; 44, 13 ; þann, Gylf. 10, 15 ; 25, 7 ; Olafs. 115, 13–14 ; þat, Gylf. 10, 8 ; 13, 6–7 ; 29, 2 ; 40, 4–5 etc., altogether 20 times ; þá, Gylf. 9, 5–6 ; 49, 1 : þær, Gylf. 22, 8 ; 45, 7 ; þenna, Gylf. 96, 1 ; Olafs. 266, 23 ; þetta, Gylf. 40, 7 ; Olafs. 271, 11 : þetta veitti sauða-maðrinn honum. Very interesting is the inversion after the adjective-pronoun þessi, the modified noun following after the subject : in Gylf. 18, 12 : ok þessi segir hón nöfn þeira. . . . (b) *nominal accusative* with or without a preced-ing adjective is found 24 times, as in Gylf. 15, 14 ; 17, 19 ; 24, 11 ; 68, 4 ; 100, 9 and so forth. Illustration : Olafs. 256, 18–19 : þessa penníngha hefir þú samandregit. . . .

(2) Or *a Dative :* (a) of *a pronoun :* honum (6), Gylf. 76, 12 ; 13, 19 ; Olafs. 137, 12 ; 124, 23–24 ; 145, 4 ; 300, 2 ; henni (2), Gylf. 34, 4 ; 42, 17 ; þeim (4), Gylf. 8, 2 ; 99, 1 ; Olafs. 274, 1 ; 294, 14 ; því (1), Gylf. 53, 4 ; and once þér (1), Olafs. 278, 4–5 : þér er nú kunnig ætt okkur ; (b) *nominal dative* with or without an attribute occurs in Gylf. 38, 21 ; 83, 4 ; 79, 12 ; Olafs. 264, 10 ; 130, 7–8 ; 145, 11–12 : konúngi gjörðist forvitni mikil ; 6 times.

(3) Or *a Genitive* (a) *pronominal :* þess, Gylf. 78, 3 ; 81, 2 ; Olafs. 143, 19 ; þessa, Olafs. 131, 25 ; þeirra, Gylf. 30, 16 : þeirra má hann eigi missa. . . . (b) *nominal genitive* modi-fied by an adjective-pronoun in Olafs. 130, 25 : þessa stríðs getr Hallfreyðr í Ólafs drápu (c) the *genitive* of the *definite article hinn* used absolutely once in Olafs. 268, 19 : enn hins vil ek eggja, at þú brennir kirkjuna. 7 cases.

(4) Or *two accusatives :* Gylf. 11, 6 : grjót ok urðir gerðu þeir af tönnum.

(5) Or *two datives:* Olafs. 264, 12 etc.: enn mér ok mínu hyski hefir hann veitt bruna. . . .

(6) Or *Nominative and Accusative*, instead of Accusative + accusative in apposition in the interesting anacoluthon of Gylf. 9, 9–10 : inn gamli hrímþuss hann köllum vér Ými. Both Wilken and Jonsson agree in the reading. Otherwise one might be tempted to read "inn gamla hrímþuss, hann . . ."

The only cases in which Inversion does *not* follow after an object are again to be found in the *poetic passages*, as in Grímnismál 14 : hálfan vál hón kyss hverjan dag, enn hálfan Óðinn á," or in Grímn. 18 "enn þat fáir vitu," or in Vafþrúðnismál 41 : vál þeir kjosa etc. In connection with this it is proper not to overlook the peculiar constructions in Gylf. 12, 11 : mikit þótti mér þeir hafa þá snúit til leiðar and, again, in Gylf. 35, 8 : allmikit þykki-mér guðin eiga undir gæzlu eða trúnaði Iðunnar etc. Are "þykki mér" and "þotti mér" verbs in the singular and thus impersonal : "methinks, methought"? Wilken, in opposition to Jonsson, as if to show how closely coupled the two words are, connects them by a dash, not only 38, 8, but also 96, 11 and 98, 20. That would leave little doubt as to his conception of the passages just quoted. But if the above-mentioned verbs are singulars and impersonal, the Old Norse order is *wrong*, according to what we said before, that after an object : mikit = Grosses and allmikit = uberaus Wichtiges inversion should follow, and, thus, the order should be : mikit þykki mér hafa þeir þá, as in German : Grosses-dünkt mich-haben sie verrichtet etc. In view of the strictness with which the law of inversion is carried through in Old Norse prose, I do not hesitate to regard the forms "þykki and þótti" as Subjunctives, in the sense of the potentialis, and as Plurals[1] at that, and consequently I look upon the above-mentioned cases as personal constructions : magna videntur mihi ei fecisse. . . .

B. *Inversion follows after a logical object in the inserted clause* without any exception, which is the rule not only in the *Germanic*, but also in the *Romance, Slavic*, and many other

---

[1] Poestion, on p. 348 of his *Einleitung in das Studium des Altnordischen*, tries to get out of the dilemma, explaining that in the 3d person singular þykki is used instead of þykkir etc. What he says about the subjunctive refers to þykki instead of þykkir.

dialects. In the *Germanic* languages the words quoted in
the oratio recta, no matter whether they reproduce the
complete statement or thought or whether they are broken
by the inserted clause, stand to the verb of the latter clause
in the relation of object + predicate, after which the subject must follow if it is expressed, as : Gylf. 59, 1, eigi þarf
ek—segir hann—at spyrja þik at nafni. " Eigi þarf ek " is
logically as well an object of " segir hann " as the whole :
" eigi þarf ek at spyrja þik at nafni." Not only the verbs
of saying, of which there are numerous cases (segja, kveða),
but also the verbs of thinking are used in such a construction : Gylf. 56, 1: fáir—vænti ek— . . . kunni segja . . .
Gylf. 26, 5 : enn ljósálfar einir—hyggjum vér—at nú
byggvi þá staði ; also Gylf. 94, 4.

C. *Inversion after Noun-Clauses* practically does not occur,
there being no instances of the substantive (or adjective)
clauses preceding an independent clause to which it stands
in relation. The only case that belongs here is Gylf. 68,
16 : enn sá er Logi heitir, þat var villieldr. But here, after
the adjective clause, the subject is for the sake of emphasis
used twice, sá and þat denoting one subject. The regular
order is natural here and is also employed in such cases in
German : "und der, welcher Logi hiess,—der or das war
das Feuer." Inversion after the Adjective-clause in a
combination of :

D. *Object + Relative Clause* is found in Olafs. 279, 3–5, and in
264, 1–3 : Alla þessa luti, er sá fjandi hafði talat, sagði
hann syni sínum. The object is given twice in Olafs. 262,
18–20 : ok alla þá luti, sem þit segit af honum, slíkt hit
sama flytr hann af ykkr. " Here, perhaps, also belongs the
peculiar anacoluthon in Gylf. 24, 7 : sú dögg (instead of þá
dogg) er þaðan af fellr á jörðina, þat kalla menn hunangs-
fall." Compare also Gylf. 9, 10.

(3) *Inversion proper*, finally, *follows after a predicate noun*, the
latter being either :

(a) *A Substantive* (42 cases) as : Gylf. 47, 9–10 : geysi mikit mein var hánum þat, so also Gylf. 14, 1 ; 14, 15 ; 27,
19 ; 50, 3 ; 50, 15 etc., etc.

(b) Or *an Adjective* (17), as : mikill er Óðinn fyrir sér, Gylf.
51, 12 ; enn meiri muntu vera, Gylf. 62, 10 ; so also 48,
2 ; 70, 4 ; 96, 1 ; Olafs. 102, 5 ; 118, 29 ; 152, 14–15 etc.
Here also belong Gylf. 42, 15 : önnur er Saga, and Gylf.
42, 16 : þriðja er Eir etc., etc., in Gylf. 27, 11 the numeral
tólf : tólf eru æsir góðkunnigir ; and also 87, 6, where the
adjective is attributive : margar eru þar vistir góðar.

(c)   Or *an Infinitive* (15 times) : enn fylgja má ek þér, Gylf.
5, 1–2 ; 47, 43 ; 52, 12 ; 61, 7 ; 82, 4 ; Olafs. 27, 2 ; 259,
13 etc., etc.

(d) Or *a Participle* (12 times) : sét muntu hafa, Gylf. 40, 2 ;
goldit var hánum þetta, Gylf. 78, 7 ; 61, 5 ; 56, 10 ; 36, 3 ;
Olafs. 130, 13 ; 305, 9–10 etc

Inversion proper in *Old Norse prose* is thus not a phenomenon
that may or may not appear, as in *Anglo-Saxon*, and, to a large
extent, in *Old Saxon* and even in *Old High German*, but it is a
law which, as in *Modern German*, is *carried through to the letter*
allowing no exceptions.   But however logical and precise, sharp
and compact the "Inversion proper" be, the language which
raises such a construction to a supreme law must suffer considerably under the disadvantage of working like a machine ; and if,
as in the case especially of *Old Norse*, the poetry breaks so often
the fetter of an order so philosophic, it is not only and exclusively
due to alliterative considerations, for the rhetorically most beauti-
ful languages are not bound by such a law.

Before closing this chapter on Inversion it must be said that if
the predicate is a compound verb, the subject—generally speaking—stands between the two constituent parts of the predicate,
as Gylf. 20, 5 : þar skulu guðin eiga dóma sína, and so forth.
But, on the other hand, there are a great many cases—at a rough
estimate about 30 per cent.—in which the subject stands after the
compound form, as Gylf. 15, 24 : þaðan eru komnir þessir úlfar ;
Olafs. 109, 15, 119, 5–6, 145, 7 etc., etc.   As regards the final
position of the compound verb in the inverted order,[1] it must
suffice to state that it is found considerably less frequently here
than in the normal order, *Old Norse*, strict as it is, preserving
thus within the province of inversion, a comparatively greater
freedom than Modern German.

---

[1] I refrain from presenting the material for the latter point as well as for the
former, because it is too voluminous, and the truth may be verified by looking
up some 3 or 4 pages.

C. RHETORICAL INVERSION.

In a treatise like this, which deals exclusively with the syntactic norm of the Old Norse order of words, the rhetorical inversion can receive but little attention, and a few remarks must suffice. On almost every page instances of inversion are found in which no verb-modifier precedes the subject. They are, indeed, so frequent as to form a secondary mode, and by no means a very unimportant one, of expressing the relation of Subject and Predicate. Ries[1] calls it "die ungerade Folge in freier Anwendung," and devotes fully 30 pages to its discussion. The rhetorical inversion extensively used in *Anglo-Saxon* and *Old High German*, and especially in the *Slavic dialects*, and appearing also in *Modern German* and *Modern English* : "Sagte der Königsson," "Said the prince,"—may in the majority of cases be reduced to the law of analogy ; in others to the omission of an understood adverbial expression of inverting power ; in others, again, to the picturesqueness and vividness of the style, which is fond of an occasional change in order to prevent monotony and to heighten the effect. The adverbial modifier of a preceding clause is so strong that its effect extends itself to the following sentences, which is without an introducing adverb : Gylf. 58, 13–14 : enn of miðja nótt varð landskjálfti mikill, gekk jörðin undir þeim skykkjum ok skalf húsit ; Gylf. 80, 9–10 : þá váru teknir synir Loka . . . brugðu æsir Vala . . . ok reif hann í sundr. In both instances there is a group of 3 sentences : the first sentence has an adverbial expression, then comes the second with the rhetorically inverted order, and is followed by ok + sentence. So further Gylf. 74, 16–17 ; 79, 11–12.

In the rapid narrative and brilliant description of the events connected with " Ragnarökr " the author has no time, as it were, to connect the actions by the calm "ok" : Gylf. 83, 11 etc. : æsirnir hervæða sik, ok sœkja fram á völluna ; ríðr fyrst Óðinn, . . . stefnir hann móti etc. etc.—In the simple enumeration as : Gylf. 10, 6 : hét einn Óðinn, annar Vili, þriðiVé ; Gylf. 13, 3 : hét karlmaðrinn Askr enn konan Embla ; so also Gylf. 13, 1–2 : gaf inn fyrsti önd, annar vit, þriði ásjónu etc., the predicate is once, at the beginning of the first sentence, emphasized and then simply omitted.

---

[1] *Quellen und Forschungen*, vol. xli., pp. 12–42.

Very frequently the adverb, instead of preceding the predicate, is found immediately after it and in front of the subject.   In such cases we may almost speak of the retroactive effect of the adverb ; as Gylf. 57, 12 : var þá annarr haltr eptra fœti ; Gylf. 79, 16–17 : ferr þá Loki fyrir netinu ; Olafs. 111, 1–2 : fór þá Ríngr konúngr aptr. . . . Olafs. 121, 9–10 : gengu síðan saman fylkíngar. . . . In Gylfag. 58, 14–17 : þá stóð þórr upp ok hét ok leituðuz ok fundu, settiz þórr. . . . further Gylf. 59, 3 ; 67, 9 etc., the "þá " is omitted.

In a few cases inversion seems to be used to indicate a causal relation : Gylf. 57, 12–14.   Thor saw it and said that the peasant or one of his family had not handled carefully the goat's bones, for he recognized : "kennir hann," at brotinn var lærleggrinn ; so also Gylf. 59, 2 etc.   The rhetorical inversion is not so frequent in the *Younger Edda* as in the *Olafssaga* and in the *Eyrbyggjasaga*. Its rhetorical effect if used for the purpose of parallelism and chiasmus is considerable.   The Old Norse independent clause, even in spite of the strictness of its "inversion proper," commands a certain freedom with which the Modern Germanic dialects cannot compare.

II. INDEPENDENT INTERROGATIVE CLAUSES.

The rules and laws which in the declarative (positive or negative) clause required an "Inversion proper," are just as valid in the interrogative sentence.   Accordingly, we should expect and we also find inversion in all cases where the interrogative word is either :

A. *An Object*, as : hvat leik vilit þér nú bjóða mér?   Gylf. 65, 21 ; or without a following noun : hvat hafðiz Allföðr?   Gylf. 17, 11 ; 29, 14–15 : hvat hafa þeir gert ?   Olafs. 134, 23 : hvern dýrökit þér?   Further illustrations are : Gylf. 6, 8 ; 8. 9 ; 29, 14 ; Olafs. 135, 3 ; 256, 17–18 ; 298, 2–3.

B. *Or an Adverb or an adverbial expression*, as : hvar er sá guð ?   Gylf. 6, 8 ; 9, 11 ; 20, 3 ; Olafs. 261, 19 ; Gylf. 12, 13 : hvaðan kómu menninir þeir ? 26, 6 ; 77, 1 ; Gylf. 9, 2 : hvernig óxu ættir þaðan ? 12, 3 ; 40, 8–9 ; 98, 21 ; Gylf. 14, 15 : hversu stýrir hann gang sólar? Gylf. 50, 14–15 : hví spyrr þú eigi þess ? 74, 11 ; 76, 22.   Olafs. 118, 19 ; 270, 18 ; Olafs. 256, 26 : fyrir hví vildir þú heldr táka af þessum penníngum ?   Gylf. 9, 11–12 : við hvat lifði hann ? 9, 15.

C. *Or a Predicate noun*, as : Olaís. 138, 6 : hver ertu ? 149, 23–24 ; Gylf. 29, 13 ; Olafs. 149, 27–28 : hvert er nafn þitt ? Gylf. 6, 21 : hvat var upphaf ? 51, 6 ; Gylf. 27, 11 : hverir eru æsir ? Gylf. 42, 13: hverjar eru Ásynjurnar ? Here also belongs the genitive qualitatis : Gylf. 96, 11–12 : hvers kyns var hann ?

The other Germanic dialects have under the same conditions also invariably inversion, and *Modern English* hardly knows of any exceptions.

As regards the position of the subject of the compound predicate, it stands in the interrogative clause always between auxiliary and verbal noun, a position in which it is not always found, as will be remembered, in the declarative sentence. Illustrations are : Gylf. 40, 8–9 : hvernig varð fjöturrinn smíðaðr ? Once, however, we read in Gylf. 97, 1–2 : "hvaðan af hefir hafiz sú íþrótt, er þér kallit skáldskap," where the position of the subject is forced to the end through the influence of the relative clause which describes the subject. Even in German such constructions are not rare under the same conditions.

If the subject is the interrogative word and opens the sentence, the order is, of course, normal : Gylf. 10, 11 ; 20, 7 ; 22, 19 ; 52, 3 : hverr á þann hest ? etc. ; or Gylf. 6, 22 : hvat var áðr ?

It is thus left for us to discuss the interrogative clauses which are not introduced by a verbal modifier or a predicate noun or a subject which is the interrogative word. All Germanic languages agree here and make the predicate, as the bearer of the most important idea, upon which naturally the main stress lies, precede the subject, which is either known already or to be known easily, and is of a relatively minor weight. *Old Norse prose* as far as examined does not show any exceptions to that rule. But there is no doubt that if in particular cases of questions the subject is relatively more important than the action, it would receive the irregular, that is, the emphatic position at the beginning of the sentence, especially in questions of surprise and considerable doubt, as in *English* and *German :* "Wilhelm hat ihn betrogen ?" etc.

Old Norse, as is well known, is fond of introducing the sentence under discussion here by the interrogative particle "hvárt," as : Gylf. 48, 11: hvárt hefir Óðinn þat sama borðhaldit ? Gylf. 59, 3 : hvárt hefir þú dregit á braut hanzka minn ? So further : Gylf. 60, 21 ; 61, 3 ; 70, 7–8 ; 77, 1–2 ; 78, 7 ; 89, 1 etc., or without an interrogative particle : Gylf. 22, 1 ; brennr eldr yfir Bifröst ? further : Gylf. 16, 7 ; 62, 9–10 ; 65, 5–6 ; 73, 3–4 ; 74, 5–7 etc. etc.

The independent *double question* is treated the same way as the *simple question*, as Gylf. 89, 1–2 : hvárt lifa nökkur guðin þá, eða er þá nökkur jörð eða himinn ? so also Gylf. 49, 6. The "eða" is not necessarily preceded by a question : as Gylf. 65, 17 ; auð- sætt er nú at máttr þinn er ekki svá mikill. . . . eða viltu freista um fleiri leika ?" so further : Gylf. 34, 9 etc. etc. etc.

III. INDEPENDENT IMPERATIVE CLAUSES.

As in the interrogative clause so also in the case of the *impera- tive clause*, the main interest concentrates itself about the verb. The subject is again well known, and for that reason not infre- quently omitted, as Gylf. 61, 11 : "hverfit aptr " instead of : "hverfit þér aptr " ; Eyrb. 107, 23 : "enda flýjum nú allir " instead of "enda flýjum vér nú allir." What Ries says about the *Heliand* is also, to a large extent, true in regard to the other *Germanic dia- lects :* "Die mit der fortschreitenden Entwickelung der Sprache zunehmende Neigung zu differenzieren, verschiedenem Inhalt auch verschiedene Form zu geben, musste die . . . abweichende Stel- lung begünstigen, welche Heische-und- Fragesatz von der breiten Masse einfacher Aussagesätze auch der äusseren Form nach abhob." [1]

We shall have to divide the imperative clauses into those of the first, second, and third persons :

A. *Imperative clauses of the first person* (Adhortativus) have the inversion without any exception, Olafs. 136, 14 : biðjum vér nú allir þann sama himna guð ; Olafs. 136, 16 : löggjumst vér niðr, etc. Here perhaps also belongs Olafs. 127, 2 : heyra viljum vér !

B. *Imperative clauses of the second person* (Command and re- quest) have always inversion, no matter whether they are or are not introduced by an adverb. Illustrations of the former charac- ter are : Olafs. 126, 14 : nú gefit þér ráð ; also Olafs. 263, 27. A conditional clause precedes + þá : Olafs. 256, 6–7 : . . . þá fá þú ok lát hann lausan. In connection with "skulu " the impera- tive occurs : Gylf. 5, 2 : skaltú þá spyrja hann nafns sjálfr, so also Gylf. 46, 21: ok nú skaltú fara ok biðja hennar mér til handa.

---

[1] *Quellen und Forsch.,* v. xli., p. 57.

Without an introducing adverb : Olafs. 104, 25 : gjörit þér allir samt þvílíkt ; Olafs. 130, 17 : hafit þér þökk ; Olafs. 137, 24 : heyr þú, Ólafr ! further : Olafs. 138, 7 ; 152, 2 ; 264, 17 ; 302, 30 ; Eyrb. 93, 21 ; Gylf. 61, 8.

If the subject of the imperative clause is strongly contrasted with another subject contained in a previous clause and is thus relatively weightier than the predicate, its emphatic position will naturally also determine its irregular position, and as the unemphatic subject follows the verb, it will now, as an emphatic subject, have to precede it : as Gylf. 59, 13, 14 : þá mælti Skrýmir til þórr, at hann vill leggjazt niðr ok sofa : enn þér takit nestbaggann ok búit til náttverðar yðr. The contrasted subject of the predicate is, as far as can be determined, in such cases always introduced by the contrasting or adversative conjunction " enn." Gylf. 34, 21–22 (in *Jonsson's* edition of the *Prose Edda*) : kunna mun ek þar af at segja, enn " þú " skalt nú fyrst heyra [1] ; further : Olafs. 280, 13 ; and finally Olafs. 305, 20–21 : nú mun ek gera bál mikit, enn " þit " þórr gángit þar at sínum megin, etc. etc.

C. *Imperative clauses of the third person* (optative) do not occur very frequently and always show inversion : Eyrb. 19, 1 : fári hann þá. The " ok " precedes, but has no influence upon the order in Gylf. 66, 18 : ok fáiz þórr við hana, and also Olafs. 297, 28 : ok fáe þeir sigr sem auþit má verða. In one instance a dependent clause precedes + þá: Gylf. 41, 4–5: enn heldr enn þér frýit mér hugar, þá leggi einhverr yðar hönd sína í munn mér. In another instance a preceding dependent clause is not followed by þá in Gylf. 66, 12–13 : svá lítinn sem þér kallit mik, gangi til einhverr ok fáiz við mik. . . .

IV. CO-ORDINATE CLAUSES.

The co-ordinate conjunctions which occur on the 200 pages that were examined for that purpose (100 pages of the *Prose Edda* and 100 of the *Olafssaga*) are: " ok," " enn," " þó," " enn þó," " heldr " ; " eigi at eins . . . heldr " ; " bæði . . . ok," " hvárki . . . né." Their influence upon the order in the co-ordinate clause is not uniform.

A) " ok." Heyse is indignant at and, in fact, attacks and condemns the *Modern German* inversion after " und," calling it

---

[1] Wilken's reading is on page 35, 10-11.

"veralterer Kanzleistil" and stating that in the better prose it affects unpleasantly the German "Sprachgefühl, und unser aesthetisches Gefühl."[1]   This view has been generally adopted by Modern Grammarians.[2] Poeschel, on the other hand, after a thorough scientific investigation comes to the result that the inversion after "und" is a phenomenon well known in the oldest stage of the language and extensively used in its other periods.[3] Mogk discussing the same subject[4] in regard to the *Scandinavian languages* says : " In der ältesten Zeit ist die Umstellung von Zeitwort und Nomen—after "ok"—durchweg neben der gewöhnlichen Wortfolge herrschend."   In regard to the " Gylfaginning " and " Bragarœður " as well as to the " Olafssaga " the statement of the distinguished scholar will need to be modified, and as 200 pages of ordinary Old Norse prose may well serve as a criterion for the whole Old Norse prose literature in a question like the one under discussion, I would differ with Mogk and venture to state that inversion after "ok" in Old Norse prose is not only "neben der gewöhnlichen Wortfolge herrschend," but, on the contrary, that *inversion* is most decidedly the *rule*, the normal order appearing only in exceptional cases.   Out of the 138 cases in the *Younger Edda*, in which "ok" introduces a co-ordinate clause containing subject and predicate, inversion is found 128 times, leaving thus only 10 illustrations of the normal arrangement ; while in the *Olafssaga* out of 109 cases 98 show inversion and 11 the normal order.   To quote here all instances of inversion seems almost impossible.   Gylf. 3, 8 : ok drógu öxninir þat land ; further illustrations for 25 pages of Gylf. are : 3, 12 ; 4,3 ; 5, 3 ; 5, 6 ; 5, 8 ; 6, 15 ; 8, 6–7 ; 8, 17 ; 8, 18–19 ; 10, 5 ; 10, 17 ; 11, 10 ; 13, 4 ; 13, 7–8 ; 13, 14 ; 14, 6 ; 14, 13 ; 14, 20 ; 15, 18 19 ; 17, 2 ; 17, 5 ; 17, 20 ; 18, 2–3 ; 20, 2 ; 20, 14 ; 22, 5 ; 22, 10 ; 23, 2 ; 24, 15 ; 25, 2–3 ; 25, 13 ; 26, 2 ; 26, 3–4 ; 27, 4 ; 27, 7 ; 27, 8 ; 27, 16 ; 28, 2–3 ; 29, 10 ; 29, 11 ; and so forth on almost every page. In Olafs. on 25 pages : 102, 28–29 : ok þökknaðist hvárt öðru vel."

---

[1] Heyse : *Deutsche Grammatik ;* Hannover, 1886, p. 274, in the elaborate Anmerkung.

[2] Also by *Whitney : German Grammar*, Revised (compendium), p. 258, special rules.

[3] In the *Einladungsschrift der Fürsten- und Landesschule in Grimma*, 1891.

[4] *Indogermanische Forschungen*, volume iv., p. 388 etc. " Inversion von Subject und Predikat in den nordischen Sprachen," deals almost exclusively with inversion after " ok."

104, 19–20 ; 105, 6–7 ; 106, 26 ; 107, 14–15 ; 107, 22 ; 109, 27 ;
110, 21 ; 113, 15 ; 114, 7 ; 116, 15 ; 116, 17–18 ; 117, 16–17 ;
118, 1 ; 118, 25 ; 118, 26 ; 119, 6 ; 121, 10 ; 121, 11 ; 121, 13 ;
121, 25–26 ; 124, 24 ; 125, 28 ; 126, 13 ; 127, 17 ; 127, 20 ; 130,
6 ; 130, 15 ; 130, 18 ; 130, 21 and so forth.

It must be remembered that "ok" has not only the simple
conjunctional force. It is, in fact, like the German "auch,"
with which it is etymologically related, much more an adverb
than a copulative conjunction, the *Old High German* "unte"
and the *Anglo-Saxon* "ond" not being truly represented at all in
Old Norse, but merely substituted by the "ok." The purely adverbial force of the "ok" is, of course, best exemplified in all
those cases in which it is not the introductory word, as Gylf.
21, 6 : hón heitir ok Ásbrú ; Gylf. 28, 1 : hann heitir ok Valföðr ; Olafs. 109, 17 : þá var ok gjör kirkja í Árósi etc. In all
these cases the "ok" could well be translated by the German
"auch," but never, of course, by the "und." It is thus not un-
safe to say that the inversion after "ok" is in by far the majority
of cases due to the universal law of *Old Norse inversion* after a
preceding adverbial expression, which the "ok" was also felt to be.

Before going over to the normal order after "ok," a few words
about *Anglo-Saxon* might not be without interest. When compared with the inversion and lack of inversion after many adverbial expressions in Anglo-Saxon, it seems that the inversion
after "ond" is not so very rare : *Anglo-Sax. Chronicle :* 709 :
ond wæs totæled . . . Westseaxna land. 836 : Ond feng Aeþel-
wulf Ecgbrehting to Westseaxna rice. 875 : Ond for Godruns.
. . . Kube calls the just quoted illustrations "einige schwer zu
erklärende Fälle der Inversion." [1]

Normal order after "ok" in the Gylf. is found in : 10, 6–7 ;
16, 1 ; 16, 3 ; 31, 7 ; 34, 7 ; 44, 6 ; 68, 3 ; 90, 1 ; 97, 9 ; 98, 13 ;
and in Olafs. 102, 5–6 ; 115, 28 ; 119, 25 ; 125, 27 ; 127, 9–10 ;
133, 8–9 ; 138, 4 ; 141, 10–11 ; 142, 8 ; 146, 7–8 ; 295, 20.

To account for the normal order after "ok" in a dogmatic
way is hardly a safe thing to do. But would not the mere statement of two or more simultaneous actions coupled together by a
co-ordinate conjunction more likely be expressed by the normal
order ? In such a case the "ok" would have a much more con-

---

[1] Emil Kube : *Die Wortstellung in der Sachsenchronik*, Jena, 1886, § 6.

junctional force than if it were used as a particle to express pro-
gression and succession of action, in which latter case its logical
force is that of an adverb.   For instance, in Gylf. 5, 1–3 : hann
svarar ok segir . . . ok sneriz sá maðr . . . the action is pro-
gressing and instead of "ok" we might as well have used : þá, or
"eptir þat."   On the other hand, in Gylf. 44, 5–6 : hón gætir dura
ok lýkr aptr . . . ok hón er sett til varnar á þingum . . . etc.
Sýn's watching the door, her closing it and her being placed
there to prevent falsehoods are, of course, not meant to be suc-
cessive actions.   The same is further true of Gylf. 16, 1 ; 16, 3 ;
31, 6–7 : hann er svá fagr ok bjartr, at . . . ok eitt gras er
svá hvitt, at . . . (perhaps here also influence of parallelism)
34, 10 : hann er djarfastr . . . ok hann ræðr ; 97, 8–9.   In other
cases, again, the subject is emphatic, and having the greater stress
it requires the prominent, irregular and emphatic position, as
Gylf. 98, 11–13 : þeir biðja Suttung ok bjóða hánum . . . til
sættar i föðurgjöld mjöðinn dýra ok "þat"—namely the offer of
the important mead—verðr at sætt með þeim ; so further in
Gylf. 10, 6 : ok þat er mín trúa, at. . . . 90, 1 : ok hitt mun þér
undarligt þykkja, er. . . . etc.   In both cases the subject in the
prominent position heightens our interest for the following dependent clause which is logically a subject.   Gylf. 68, 3 is perhaps a dependent clause.   What has been said about the normal
order after "ok" in *Gylfag.* is also true in regard to the *Olafssaga.*

B) "enn" in 118 out of 122 cases in the *Younger Edda* requires
the normal order, as Gylf. 3, 4 : enn sú kona var ein af ása-ætt, so
further : 3, 7 ; 6, 17 ; 8, 18 ; 9, 8 ; 9, 13 ; 15, 17 ; 17, 7 ; 20, 1 ; 20,
12 ; 20, 17 ; 24, 15 ; 30, 3 ; 30, 8 and so forth.   In the *Olafssaga*
all the 90 instances show normal arrangement, as 102, 1 : enn ek
segi þat, further 111, 6 ; 113, 11–12 ; 115, 1–2 ; 121, 24–25 ; 123,
20 ; 126, 16 ; 127, 5 ; 130, 17 ; 133, 9–10 etc.

In regard to the inversion after "enn," which occurs 4 times
in Gylf. 23, 11 : enn er þat sagt ; 28, 4 : ok enn hefir hann
nefnz á fleiri vega ; 66, 16 and 69, 3 : ok enn mælti hann, it
must be said that the "enn" seems to mean, "moreover, further,
besides," being thus strictly adverbial in force.   In the latter
meaning it occurs frequently in the middle of the sentence, as
in Gylf. 23, 10 : svá er enn sagt ; Olafs. 130, 8 : ok spurði enn
Óla, and so forth.

C) "þó," generally found in connection with "ok" or "enn," is a conjunctional adverb in character and thus always takes inversion, as Gylf. 67, 20 : enn þó veit ek ; 29, 5 : enn þó er þer þat skjótast at segja ; further : 40, 18 ; 64, 19 ;—In Olafs. "þó" introduces more frequently a clause, as 305, 30 : ok þó geng ek til þessa prófs. . . . 133, 11–12 : enn þó hugfesti hann, etc. ; further 135, 11 ; 138, 1–2 ; 146, 18 ; 288, 23 ; 298, 11 ; 303, 5 ; 305, 27 ; 306, 17–18. . . .

D) "heldr," being also essentially conjunctional adverbial, requires inversion in Gylf. 54, 14 : heldr synjaði hann hánum at byggva. . . . The clause preceding it is negative. As a second member of the combination :

E) "eigi at eins . . . heldr" it also requires inversion in Olafs : 267, 1 : eigi at eins þar í næstum sveitum, heldr fóru þeir víða um Ísland ; and 281, 20–21 : eigi at eins stundligu ríki, heldr gerir hann sína þræla bræðr síns, etc.

F) "bæði . . . ok" is found in Olafs. 155, 19–20 : bæði var hann hárr ok digr, in which the "bæði" is followed by inversion while the "ok" connects only a predicate adjective.

G) "hvárki . . . né" is used in *Jonsson's Edition of the Edda :* 41, 10 : hvárki svaf hann né drakk. Wilken reads : 46, 11 : ekki svaf hann, ekki drakk hann. . . .

Summing up the order of words after the co-ordinate particles, we find that only "enn" requires the normal arrangement, while the other particles, with a few exceptions after "ok," are followed by inversion. In *Old Norse*, then, it would seem that the only co-ordinate conjunction pure and simple, without any admixture of adverbial force, is "enn," while the remaining particles, as is frequently the case with the German "doch, jedoch, also, auch,"[1] are regarded as adverbial conjunctions or conjunctional adverbs.

V. DEPENDENT CLAUSES.

As regards the dependent clauses, Old Norse is comparatively free, much more so than any other Early Teutonic dialect. In *Anglo-Saxon*, in by far the majority of cases, 82 per cent if the verb is simple,[2] the predicate holds an extreme end position as in *Modern German*, an order which is better known as "*transpo-*

---

[1] Heyse : *Deutsche Grammatik*, page 275, 3. Anmerkung.
[2] *Modern Lang. Associat. Publications*, 1893, p. 229.

sition." In *Old-Saxon* has " die verschiedene Behandlung, die die Stellung des Verbs zu den übrigen Satzgliedern erfährt . . . sich allmälig zum wesentlichen, für die beiden Satztypen characteristischen Artunterschied herausgebildet." [1] *Gothic* occasionally shows independently of the *Greek original* the extreme end-position of the auxiliary verb ; for instance, almost always in the phrase : hausideduþ þatei quiþan ist, Matth. 5, 43 etc., for which the Greek has the Aorist Passive,[2] but also in the independent clause the auxiliary is, in opposition to the original, at liberty to follow the verbal noun : ni nauhþanuh galagiþs vas, John 3, 24 ; etc.   Becker[3] remarks that the transposed order appears as a law all through *Old High German* literature and that exceptions are very rare.   In view of a law which may be styled typically *Germanic*, it is rather strange and interesting to observe that the Old Norse by no means shares, generally speaking, the fondness for the transposed order of the dialects just mentioned.   On the contrary, it treats its dependent clauses very much like its independent clauses, preserving for the transposed order a proportionately insignificant amount of dependent clauses.   The most important orders are thus the "normal" and the "inverted" arrangements.   In the latter order, however, we have to discriminate between (1) inversion caused by a subordinate conjuntion only, an order which is employed very rarely and only for rhetorical considerations—being bound and subject to no laws and rules —as a mere variety and deviation from the normal monotony ; and (2) inversion caused by some word modifying the predicate of the dependent clause, a phenomenon so familiar in the *Old Norse independent clause*, as an order to be strictly observed and followed.   The most convenient way of discussing the order of words in dependent clauses is to consider the normal and inverted arrangements, with all the peculiarities and exceptions, in one chapter, and the transposed order in another.

A. *Dependent Normal and Inverted Orders.*

If a subordinate conjunction introduces the dependent clause, the order is, generally speaking, normal : x + Subject + predicate ; all dependent clauses sharing equally in that arrangement.

---

[1] *Quellen und Forschungen*, v. 41, p. 67.

[2] ἠκούσατε οὐκ ἐρρήθη.

[3] Becker's *Deutsche Grammatik*, p. 436.

If the predicative combination is expressed by *copula plus predicate noun*, the latter follows the copula, as in the independent clauses, no matter whether it is a substantive or an adjective. If the predicate verb is modified by an *adverb* or by an *adverbial expression*, the latter is bound to the position after the modified verb, as Gylf. 15, 13 : þó at hón fari ákafliga ; 40, 1 : þóttu vitir eigi áðr. . . . Olafs. 131, 12 : ok herjaði hvar sem hann kom við land. The *object* is no less strictly bound to that law than is the adverbial modifier : Gylf. 38, 6 : at hón skyldi skipta öllum vistum ; Gylf. 40, 20 : þótt ek slíta í sundr svá mjótt band ; Olafs, 110, 19 : enn er Íngjaldr spurði þat. Olafs. 111, 6 : til er þeir fundu Gorm konúng.

If the predicate is a *compound tense* of the verb and is modified by an *adverb* or an *adverbial expression*, the same tendency prevails as in the independent clause to place them frequently between auxiliary and verbal noun : as Gylf. 79, 1 : svá sem net er síðan gört ; 79, 8 : at þat mundi vél vera ; 89, 10 : er fyrrum höfðu verit ; 94, 6 : . . . at Loki skal aldri lauss verða ; Olafs. 127, 6 : . . . at ek man hér leggja. . . . 139, 8–9 : . . . at hann mætti þar grundvalla guðs kristni. The intermediate position is, of course, not obligatory, and, as in the independent clause, the adverbial modifiers are not infrequently placed after the modified verb : Olafs. 135, 18 : þá er Ólafr hafði verit 3 vetr á Vindlandi ; 139, 6 : at hann mundi fara í Garða ríki ; Gylf. 68, 2–3 : ef ek hefða vitat áðr. . . . 73, 14–15 : . . . at hann skyldi standa upp á þingum. . . .

If the *dependent compound verb* is modified by an *object*, the latter shows the same inclination as the adverbial modifier to be placed between the constituent parts of the predicate : Olafs. 138, 16 : sem hann hafði þessa luti séð ok heyrt . . . 139, 26 : þau er mega öðrum nökkura hjálp veita ; 140, 3–4 : furr enn ek hefir yðr, konúngr, ok allan þenna lýð leidt . . . 140, 28 : þegar hann mátti nökkut atfærast. Olafs. 141, 8–9 : at móðir yður man þenna mann hafa fyrirsjeth forðum daga ; Olafs. 146, 24 : at þessi maðr mundi honum sanna luti sagt hafa, etc. The object is, of course, not bound to precede the verbal noun, but may just as well, although less frequently, follow it : Olafs. 139, 14 : . . . at konúngr lét stefna fjölmennt þing ; Olafs. 141, 13 : sá er . . . mundi prýða þetta ríki. . . . Olafs. 141, 19–20 : at údygð mundi undir búa okkrum kærleikum. Olafs. 142, 11 : at hann mætti njóta þeirra góðgernínga etc. . . .

In regard to the *negation* "*eigi*" [1] in the dependent clause it must be said that, as a rule, it partakes of the most decided tendency of the adverb to follow the word it modifies, if the dependent verb is in a simple tense : Gylf. 8, 5 : þá er sá íss . . . rann eigi ; 40, 1 : þóttu vitir eigi. . . . Gylf. 51, 7 : er þeir drekka eigi ; 65, 1–2 : at stikillinn vill eigi . . . 65, 10 : ef þú gerir eigi . . . 69, 15. . . . at þér komit eigi, . . . 74, 12 : því at ek sé eigi.   The negation in front of the dependent verb is, in the normal order, rare : Gylf. 47, 9 : at hann eigi átti . . . 62, 12 : sá er eigi kunni . . . and finally, *perhaps*, 93, 17 : at eigi soðnaði.   If the dependent predicate is a verb in a compound tense, the negation is in by far the majority of cases, in 21 out of 22, placed between auxiliary and verbal noun, never after the compound verb : Gylf. 29, 11– 12 : ef þú skalt eigi kunna frásegja ; 34, 19 : enn þá er æsir vildu eigi leysa hann ; 39, 6 : ef slík stórsmíði mætti eigi halda hánum ; 39 16 : at þeir mundu eigi fá bundit úlfinn ; 40, 6 : er þú mátt eigi reyna ; 40, 24 : enn ef þú fær eigi þetta band slitit ; further : 41, 1–2 ; 46, 21 ; 56, 5 ; 56, 13 ; 56, 16 ; 57, 13 ; 59,19 ; 64, 19 ; 66, 9 ; 67, 7 ; 68, 21 ; 77, 15–16 ; 78, 6–7 ; 96, 3.   Only once " eigi " stands in the normal order between subject and auxiliary : Gylf. 44, 6 : þeim er eigi skulu inn ganga.

It hardly need be said that, for the sake of emphasis, any modifier may be taken out of its normal place, and we shall see later on what changes the irregular position of said verb-modifiers brings about in dependent clauses.

Summing up all possible combinations in the normal order of dependent clauses, of 1 subject, 1 verb, verb-modifier, we receive the following table :

A. Dependent Simple Predicate Verb.

(1) Conjunction or x + subject + verb.

(2) Conjunction or x + subject + verb+ verb-modifier.

(3) Conjunction or x + subject + copula + predicate substantive.

(4) Conjunction or x + subject + copula + predicate adjective.

(5) Conjunction or x + subject + copula + predicate substantive + verb-modifier.

(6) Conjunction or x + subject + copula + predicate adjective + verb-modifier.

---

[1] The remarks on " eigi " are based upon *Gylfaginning*.

B. Dependent Compound Predicate Verb.

(1) Conjunction or x + subject + auxiliary + verbal noun.

(2) Conjunction or x + subject + auxiliary + auxiliary infinitive + verbal noun.

(3) Conjunction or x + subject + auxiliary + verbal noun + auxiliary infinitive.

(4) Conjunction or x + subject + auxiliary + verb-modifier + verbal noun.

(5) Conjunction or x + subject + auxiliary + verbal noun + verb-modifier.

(6) Conjunction or x + subject + auxiliary + verb-modifier + verbal noun + verb-modifier.

(7) Conjunction or x + subject + auxiliary + verbal noun + predicate noun or adjective.

(8) Conjunction or x + subject + auxiliary + predicate noun or adjective + verbal noun.

There is no deviation from the normal order, if the dependent clause has *two* or more *predicates* and *one subject ;* or *two or more subjects* and *one predicate ;* or, finally, *two* or more *subjects* and *two* or more *predicates.* The tables for the independent clauses may be consulted for that purpose, with the understanding, of course, that in each case the conjunction or x precedes the subject.

(1) *Substantive Clauses.*

(a) *indirect declarative* : after verbs of saying, thinking, believing, after verbs of direct perception and after simple introductory expressions have all the normal order : svá er sagt, at Loðbrókar synir hafi rekit mestan hernað í forneskiu . . . Olafs. 114, 24–25; þótti heiðíngjum . . ., at goðin voru reið Stefni . . Olafs. 286, 13–14 ; ek veit, at sá guð er máttigr . . . Olafs. 136, 10–11 ; þá bar, at þeir vildu ríða til várþings í Hegranes . . . Olafs. 273, 3–4. Only once is there an inversion without anything to account for it in Eyrb. 5, 25–26 : ok sá þeir, at skárust í landit inn firðir stórir ; while on the other hand, in all cases where by emphasis the modifier of the dependent predicate verb or copula is torn from its regular position after the verb, and placed at the beginning of the clause immediately after the subordinating conjunction, *Inversion* appears as a strict rule with almost no exceptions. As a list of all the verb-

modifiers requiring inversion in the dependent clause, irre-
spective of the character of such a clause, will be added to
this chapter, a few illustrations must do in each case, and
as many illustrations will be given as are essential for the
establishment of the principle in all its bearings. Olafs.
125, 19–20 : hann spurði, at þar var fyrir Ottó ; Gylf. 5,
15 : hann svarar, at fyrst vil hann vita . . . Gylf. 39, 7–8 :
úlfrinn hugsaði, at hánum hafði afl vaxit. Gylf. 64, 13–14
. . . ok hyggr, at eigi skal hann þurfa optar at lúta í hornit.
Olafs. 295, 18 : nú hefi ek heyrt, at víða um heiminn sé
haldinn annar siðr. Gylf. 68, 21 : enn þat veit trúa mín,
at þá varð þat undr, etc., and finally Gylf. 16, 9 : kann vera
at þat kallir þú regnboga. Nothing could be more precise
and definite. All the *various modifiers* which require inversion in the independent clause have the same *inverting
power* in the *dependent* one, no matter whether it is an
object or an *adverbial expression*, or a *predicate noun, adjective, infinitive* or *participle*.

(b) *indirect interrogative clauses* after verbs of inquiry, report,
thinking, believing have all the normal order : hví spyrr
þú eigi þess hversu margar dyrr eru á höllini, Gylf. 50,
14–15 ; . . . fur skömmu var mér sagt, hverr þú vart ok
hverr þú munt verða, Olafs. 148, 2–3, which as the direct
question would be : hverr ertu ok hverr muntu verða?
þorvaldr segir, hvat hann hafði gert, Olafs. 270, 17–18 ;
direct : hvat hefir þú gert ? hún vildi kjör af hafa, hvern
hún skyldi eiga af þeim mönnum, Olafs. 149, 10 : direct :
hvern skal ek eiga ? enn þat þótti ásum mikit undr, hversu
stór björg sá hestr dró, Gylf. 53, 7 ; hann hl´ddi, ef hann
næmi nökkur orðaskil, Eyrb. 13, 1. While in the latter
instance, which is introduced by a conjunction only, the
normal order would be natural and expected, according to
the rule that a mere subordinate conjunction requires
normal order, we should expect, on the other hand, that in
dependent interrogative clauses introduced by an object,
or a predicate noun or an adverbial expression as *the interrogative words*, inversion would follow, as it does in
almost every such case. But if there were no such external differentiation, we could not possibly discriminate between an independent and dependent interrogative clause,

and this is, perhaps, the only, although logically the most natural, case where Old Norse prose becomes inconsistent in the strictness of its use of inversion. The instance which might be called an exception is found in Gylf. 4, 4–5, in the dependent double question : ok hugsaði hann hvárt þat mundi vera af eðli sjálfra þeirra, eða mundi því valda guðmögn, after which a relative clause describing the "guðmögn" follows, the subject being thus forced to the end position for stilistic reasons. On the other hand, the several instances of *Inversion* in the dependent interrogative clauses all show that the *verb-modifier* which caused the inverted order in each case is *not the interrogative word*, but, on the contrary, that the interrogative word precedes such modifiers : Gylf. 67, 17 : ok spyrr, hvernig hánum þykkir ferð sín orðin ; "hvernig" is the interrogative word which precedes the object "hánum," the modifier which requires inversion ; but immediately after that we read : eða hvárt hann hefir hitt ríkara mann etc. ; so also Olafs. 146, 28 : spurði hann, hvaðan honum kom sú speki ; Olafs. 284, 5 : konúngr frétti, ef honum væri hugr . . . further : Eyrb. 21, 25–26 : Oddr spyrr, hvárt hrossum höfðu stolit útlendir menn ; Eyrb. 97, 4–5 ; and Gylf. 5, 17, and finally Gylf. 90, 4–5 : veit ek eigi, hvaðan þér kemr þat.

(c) *indirect imperative-optative clauses,* after verbs of command, volition, desire, etc., are always expressed by the normal order : Olafs. 139, 3 : síðan bað hann biskup þann . . . . at hann færi í Garðaríki, . . . 136, 14–15 : biðjum vér nú, at hann skýli oss fyrir sitt krossmark. Eyrb. 93, 12 : enn þuríðr vildi, at hón færi þangat. There is no case of inversion where the subordinate clause is introduced by a dependent particle only, but, again, if the particle is followed by some modifier of the dependent predicate, *Inversion* appears, as always : Olafs. 279, 27–26 : it was agreed, at þessu boði skulu þeir í móti standa . . . Olafs. 297, 25, Eyrb. 16, 14–15 : and the stipulation was, at þá skyldi þegar upp gjalda féit ; further Olafs. 296, 25–26 : it is my request, at þenna mann lokkit þér með . . . fögrum orðum, and finally Gylf. 27, 2 : I prefer, at heldr spyrir þú eitt sinn ófróðliga.

(2) *Adjective clauses.* Although the relative clauses have considerably more cases of transposition than any other kind of dependent clauses, it is nevertheless safe to say that the normal order is the general mode of expressing it, over 70 per cent of the relative clauses being treated that way. If the relative word is simply an object case of " er " inversion is not used, unless there be some modifier of inverting power after the relative object. Not even after the relative introducer " sem " or " er " depending on a post-positive preposition does inversion take place : " and she invites you " í höfuðborg þessa ríkis, " sem " hún séalf sitr " í," Olafs. 102, 18 ; sá guð, er alla luti hefir skapat, Olafs. 127, 13–14 ; and 127, 15 : sínu eyrendi, því " sem " þèr farit " með." Olafs. 259, 18–19 : . . . þessi maðr, " er " hann sagði svá mikla frægð " af." Olafs. 112, 8–9 : ok kallaði Knút af knúti þeim, " er " (Obj.) barnit hafði með sér, so further Olafs. 101, 27 : nema þau " er " (Obj.) þú hefir frétt, etc. If " er " is object, the predicate precedes the subject only if the latter is forced to the end position by an apposition or by adverbial expressions, appositive in character, as Olafs. 255, 16 : þeirra dóttir var þorlaug, er átti Guðmundr hinn ríki á Möðruvöllum ; or Eyrb. 8, 19 : Gerðr var dóttir, er átti þormóðr goði, son Odds hins rakka ; so further Eyrb. 9, 21 ; 9, 23 etc. Neither the " er " nor the " sem," although logically objects, have, as remarked above, strange as it may seem, in themselves inverting power. The constant use in *Old Norse* of " er " and " sem " as pure *subordinate conjunctions* after which no inversion follows, is perhaps the reason why the same words used relatively as objects were not felt to be true objects with the power of inversion, especially since as relative pronouns they lacked all inflection and external indication of the oblique case. But if the relative pronouns are followed by some word modifying the dependent predicate, the latter, of course, precedes the subject, that is, *Inversion* takes place, as Gylf. 9, 3 : trúi-þér þann guð, er nú sagðir þú frá ? Gylf. 97, 8 : spyrr hann þeirra hluta, er eigi kann hann orlausn, or Olafs. 114, 20–21 : . . . Englands, er áðr höfðu átt hans ættmenn ok frændr, etc. Other cases are : Gylf. 12, 2 ; 32, 9 ; Olafs. 110, 25 ; 115, 23 ; 117, 20 ; 120, 5 ; 279, 6 ; 279, 8 ; Eyrb. 91, 18.

(3) *Adverbial clauses :*

(a) *Local* adverbial clauses all have normal order : Gylf. 3, 11 ;
þar sem landit hafði upp gengit. Gylf. 71, 6–7 : þá sneriz
þórr á braut þangat, er hann sá öxnaflokk nökkurn. Gylf.
98, 23 : ok kam þar, er þrælar slógu hey. Olafs. 131, 12 :
ok herjaði hvar sem hann kom við land, etc. What has been
said about the "er" and "sem" in the adjective-clause
used objectively is also true if the same words are used
adverbially. As introducers of a dependent clause they
have lost the inverting power, and *Inversion* is used only if
the local adverb of the relative clause is followed by some
modifier of the predicate of the dependent clause, as Eyrb.
104, 20, Gylf. 89, 6 : ok byggja þeir á Iðavelli, þar sem fyrr
var Ásgarðr, further also Gylf. 20, 10 : enn önnur er með
hrím-þussum, þar sem forðum var Ginnunga-gap. Not
counted here are the familiar clauses. . . . "þar, sem
heitir Gimlé, or þar sem heitir á Kjallarst," in which cases
the subject is omitted.

(b) *Temporal adverbial clauses* have almost exclusively the
normal order, if there is nothing to prevent it, as Gylf. 4,
9 : ok er hann kom inn í borgina, etc., or 13, 9 : ok þá er
Óðinn settiz þar í hásæti ; 7, 14, etc., hversu skipaðiz,
áðr enn ættirnar yrði eða aukaðiz mannfólkit. Here the
second clause after "eða" is inverted, so also after "ok"
in Gylf. 17, 1–2 : þá mun hón brotna þá er Múspells megir
fara at herja . . . ok svima hestar þeira yfir stórar ár.
Other temporal conjunctions are "meðan" in Olafs. 305,
4–5 : . . . meðan hann heldr trúlyndi við mik ; and
"þegar", in Olafs. 306, 28 : þegar er konúngr fór út ór
firði. The temporal clauses are, of course, very numerous.
Inversion occurs, again, in all cases where the temporal
particle precedes a modifier of the dependent predicate
verb or copula : enn er "þetta" (Obj.) spurðu landsmenn,
Olafs. 118, 5 ; enn er "bóndum (Obj.) kom þingboð
konúngs, Olafs. 279, 20–21 ; áðr enn "sagt" (pred. partc.)
er allt þat, Gylf. 31, 1 ; 79, 10 ; enn þá er "full" (pred.
adj.) er munnlaugin, Gylf. 80, 17 ; and finally Eyrb. 18, 24:
ok er mjök (adverb) leið á kveldit.

(c) *Modal-comparative clauses* (*of manner and degree*) have
normal order, unless prevented by well-known reasons.

Gylf. 79, 1: tók hann língarn ok reið á ræksna svá sem net er síðan gört.   Olafs. 138, 14–15 : ok muntu . . . öðlast meiri dyrð, enn þú hefir nú séð hér.   Olafs. 254, 9–11 : Ólafr heiti ek . . . sem þú munt heyrt hafa getit.   In the conditional-modal sense "sem" is used in Olafs. 290, 5: þórólfr . . . elskaði hann, sem hann væri hans son ; and so forth.   As in all clauses *Inversion* is caused by the fact that the modifier of the dependent predicate is removed from its normal place, so in Olafs. 118, 28 : svá drúpir nú Danmerk, sem dauðr (pred. adj.) sé Knútr ; Olafs. 263, 18 : . . . sem furr (Adv.) var hann vanr ; Eyrb. 98, 2 : . . . sem þá (adv.) var siðr ; Gylf. 40, 11 :   . . . sem nú (adv.) skaltu heyra ; Gylf. 40, 19–20 : "methinks, as if, sem önga frægð (object) muna ek af hljóta ; so further Gylf. 56, 9 etc.

(d) *Causal clauses* are also expressed by the normal order, as Olafs. 102, 14 : fyrir því at þér farit með friði. . . . Gylf. 43, 9 ; er sú sök til þess, at hón gaf sér ýmis heiti, . . . sometimes "er" is used as causal particle : Gylf. 22, 14 ; 34, 8 ; 47, 6 ; þessi sök var til, er Freyr var svá vápnlauss, . . . so also Gylf. 69, 10 ; sometimes "sem " is used in the same sense : Gylf. 75, 2–3 : Óðinn bar þeim mun verst þenna skaða, sem hann kunni mesta skyn. . . . Gylf. 78, 5–6 : almiklu kom Loki á leið. . . . því er hann varð eigi leystr frá Helju.—Here again, *Inversion* is used under the well known condition that the modifier of the dependent verb shall be placed directly after the causal particle, as Gylf. 26, 21. . . . því at þetta (obj.) vitu allir menn ; Gylf. 28, 1 : hann heitir ok Valföðr því at hans óskasynir (pred. noun) eru allir þeir, etc.   Gylf. 82, 5–6 ; þá geysiz hafit. . . . fyrir því at þá (adv.) snýz Miðgarðsormr í jötunmóð, so also Eyrb. 84, 6–7 ; 96, 29–30 ; Eyrb. 95, 17–18 : þvíat mér (Dative) segir svá hugr um ; Olafs. 258, 29. . . . þvíat litlu áðr hafði hann hertekna sonu þessa sama hertoga leyst. . . . etc., etc.

(e) *Final clauses* (*purpose*) are expressed in the normal order, as Olaf. 127, 13 : I advise to fast in order that . . . til þess at sá guð gefi oss at sigrast á Dönum. . . . Gylf. 78, 11 : gerði þar hús ok fjórar dyrr, at hann mátti sjá ór húsinu í allar ættir, and one more illustration : Eyrb. 12,

1 : enn til þess, at þeir væri vel sáttir ok vinir þaðan af, þá gjörði hann, etc., etc. *Inversion* is, of course, used if the final particle is followed by a word modifying the dependent predicate, as : Gylf. 24, 2–3 : . . . til þess, at eigi (Neg.) skyli limar hans tréna eða fúna. Gylf. 69, 7 : ok vannz hánum lengð til at jörðina (Obj.) tæki sporðr ok höfuð, and, finally, Gylf. 73, 10 : Frigg tók svardaga til þess at eira (pred. inf.) skyldu Baldri eldr ok vatn.

(f) *Consecutive-Result-Clauses* are treated like the other clauses. If there is nothing to prevent it, the normal order follows : as Olaf. 108, 7 : þeir skiptu ríki með sér svá at Lotharíus hafði Burgundíam ; Olafs. 138, 26 : ok svá fékk honum mikils, at hans augu vóru full af tárum ; Eyrb. 84, 19 : þá vóru sár hans mjök gróinn, svá at hann var vel vápnfærr ; Gylf. 14, 17 : þau váru svá fögr, at hann kallaði son sinn Mána. In Olafs. 154, 18 : þá dreif lið til Haralds konúngs, svá at sveinn varð borinn ofrliði ok flýði hann, inversion follows after the "ok"; rather peculiar is the passage Olafs. 263, 27 : nú gjör þú svá mannliga at þú rek þá brottu, the order of which is normal, the verb "rek" being in the imperative form, and being, further, preceded by a subordinate conjunction. One is reminded here of the famous Gothic "saihvei ei saihvei," in which the second predicate is also preceded by an apparently dependent particle, although it will be remembered that both Braune and Douse treat the "ei" from an entirely different standpoint. As regards the *Inverted* order of the consecutive clause, it appears here under the same premises as everywhere else : namely, if the subordinate conjunction is followed by a modifier of the dependent predicate ; as Gylf. 42, 10 : svá mikils virðu guðin vé sín, at eigi (Adv.) vildu þau saurga þá með blóði úlfsins. Olafs. 105, 4–5 : hann veitti atsókn . . . svá harða, at á skamri stundu (adv. phrase) brutu þeir. . . ; Olafs. 118, 24–25. . . . komu margar krákur ok plokkaðu hann svá, at af honum (prepos. + case) eru allar fjaðrar ; Eyrb. 96, 17 : sótti hón þá svá fast, at honum (object) gékzt hugr við Olafs. 128, 16 : . . . svá at um morgininn eptir (Adverbial phrase + adverb) sá engi líkindi Danavirkis. . . . Twice, however, in *Gylfaginning Inversion* occurs without regard to the well-

established rule: 57, 20 : hann herði hendrnar á hamar-
skaptinu, svá at hvítnuðu knúarnir ; and 89, 15 : af þessum
mönnum kemr svá mikil kynslóð, at byggviz heimr allr ;
they are very exceptional cases : in the former instance the
rhetorical stress lies on the impressive verb ; in the latter
on the subject, and the emphatic position—which is iden-
tical with the uncommon and irregular one—removed the
verb from its normal second to its irregular first place, and
the subject from its normal first to its unusual second place.

(g) *Concessive clauses*, also, generally have the normal order :
Gylf. 15, 13. . . . þó at hón fári ákafliga ; Gylf. 40, 1: þóttu
vitir eigi áðr þessi tíðindi ; Gylf. 27, 14 : ok svá sem önnur
guðin eru máttug ; Olafs. 278, 5 : þóat þú hafir eigi verit lengi
í þessu landi ; Olafs. 294, 4 : . . . þóat sveinninn væri bundinn við skipit ; Eyrb. 100, 7 : þóat menn væri skírðir. . . .
Here, again, as in the other dependent clauses, *Inversion* is
employed only under the condition that the verb modifier
be torn from its regular position after the predicate ; as
Gylf. 42, 11 : þótt svá segi spárnar ; Olafs. 291, 28 : þóat
eigi þurfti avlit inn at bera, and the illustration in Olafs.
104, 5-7 : . . . þóat eptir boði náttúrunnar (in the course
of nature, of time) hafi farsælan oss lengi fylgjusavm
verit ; so further Gylf. 40, 5-6 ; Eyrb. 11, 23 ; 95, 10-11 ;
in Olafs. 294, 6, the inversion takes place contrary to the
rule : Rögnvaldr hafði svá um búit, at hann mátti eigi leysa
sik, at þó vóru lausar hendr hans. . . . ; it will be noticed
that instead of þóat or þótt, the usual concessive particle,
we have here : at þó ; but whether the inversion is due to
that change is an entirely different question, which I dare
not answer.   Very peculiar and interesting is the inversion
in Olafs. 300, 29-30 : enn sá guð er svá máttugr, at hann
þvær af manninum í skírninni allar syndir, " aldri hefir hann
áðr svá ilt gört " = habe er auch noch so Böses je vorher
gethan ; although this is, to my mind, the only way to
translate it, one thing is especially perplexing : the strange
indicative of " hafa " instead of the subjunctive which is
used in the kindred dialects.   The " aldri," too, at the beginning seems no less out of place.   It may be an awkward
attempt at a construction so familiar in English and especially in German.

(h) *Conditional clauses* have almost always the normal order.
They may be introduced by "ef." . . . Gylf. 52, 15 . . .
ef hann fengi gert borginn á einum vetri ; or by " útan " :
Olafs. 129, 12: útan þér sýnit þar með opinber tákn ; or by
"nema ": Olafs. 259, 4 : nema Sveinn konúngr væri útleystr
ok frelstr með öllum mönnum; or simply by "at" as in Gylf.
15, 12: eigi mundi hón þá meir hvata göngunni, at hón hrædd-
diz bana sinn ; sometimes by "at " following an expression
of condition : Olafs. 305, 30 etc.: ok þó geng ek . . . með
þeim skildaga at hvárgi . . . skal öðrum hjálpa ; sometimes, further, by "er": Eyrb. 22, 30 ; Olafs. 271, 24 :
"especially if " = . . . allra helzt er hann hefir heilsamligri
skilníng á sínu ráði, enn frændr hans. In Gylf. 67, 23,
etc.: ok ef ek lifi ok megak ráða, etc., the "ok" in the dependent clause requires inversion, while *once*, in Gylf. 93,
18, the *condition itself* is expressed by the *inverted order*
without any particle : vilit þér gefa mér fylli mína af uxanum
þá mun soðna á seyðinum. . . . On the other hand, *Inversion* here, as in every other dependent clause, is bound
to take place if a modifier of the dependent predicate appears right after the subordinating particle : Gylf. 42, 9 :
. . . ef þeim er ills af hánum ván ; Olafs. 258, 4 ; Eyrb. 90,
27 ; 90, 29 : ef honum væri nökkut gjört til úfriðar. Gylf.
49, 11 ; Eyrb. 95, 13 : ef eigi eru rammar skorður við
reistar. . . .

Summing up all the circumstances under which Inversion must
take place in the dependent clauses in *Old Norse prose*, we receive
the following list, which it may be interesting to compare with the
one given under the heading of "Inversion proper" in independent clauses.

I. *An Adverb, an Adverbial phrase or an Adverbial clause* preceded
by a dependent conjunction, relative pronoun or interrogative word, invariably causes inversion.

A. *Adverb.*
(1) *loci :* þar (10 times) : Olafs. 125, 19–20 ; 150, 7 ; 300, 12 ;
Eyrb. 15, 11–12 ; 14, 25 ; 85, 9–10, 95, 19 ; Gylf. 9, 12 ;
48, 1 ; 54, 11 ; hér (1) : Olafs. 102, 11–12 ; upp (1) :
Gylf. 3, 8 ; Eyrb. 88, 12–13 ; fjarri (1) : Gylf. 39, 13 ;

þangat (1): Eyrb. 6, 28. . . . (2) *temporis :* þá (12):
Olafs. 139, 2; 265, 11; 297, 27; Gylf. 68, 21; 69, 24;
70, 13; 82, 5–6; 81, 7–8; Eyrb. 16, 14–15; 96, 29–30;
98, 2; 100, 4–5; nú (5): Gylf. 9, 3; 12, 2; 40, 11;
Eyrb. 6, 24; 90, 13; æ (1): Olafs. 296, 18; áðr (1):
Olafs. 114, 20–21, aldri (3): Gylf. 60, 15; Olafs. 126, 25;
281, 24; fyrr (2): Gylf. 89, 6; Olafs. 263, 18; fyrir (1):
Eyrb. 104, 20; fyrst (1): Gylf. 5, 15; forðum (1): Gylf.
20, 10; (3) *negation :* ei (1): Olafs. 259, 9–10; ekki (3):
Gylf. 63, 14; 60, 5; 65, 18; eingi (1): Gylf. 70, 2–3;
engi (3): Gylf. 72, 10; 31, 11; 46, 20; eigi (15): Gylf.
67, 19; 72, 2; 64, 13–14; 69, 13; 97, 8; 24, 2–3; 49,
11; 29, 28; 42, 20; 48, 5; 89, 4; Eyrb. 21, 20; 97, 4–5;
95, 13; 18, 15; (4) *miscellaneous adverbs :* svá (2): Gylf.
82, 2; 42, 11; heldr (2): Gylf. 27, 2; Olafs. 296, 27;
helzt (1): Gylf. 64, 3; mjök (1): Eyrb. 18, 24; meirr
(1): Eyrb. 22, 29; ákafligast (1): Gylf. 65, 12; víðar
(1): Eyrb. 22, 21; (5) *prepositional adverbs :* gögnum (1):
Gylf. 99, 22; á (2): Gylf. 53, 12; Olafs. 121, 12. (6)
several adverbs : litlu áðr (1): Olafs. 258, 29; nökkuru
síðar (1): Gylf. 54, 17–18. . . .

B. *Adverbial phrase :*
  (1) *loci :* eptir sálinum (1): Gylf. 88, 7; (2) *temporis :* á
  skamri stundu (1): Olafs. 105, 415; á einu kveldi (1):
  Olafs. 112, 29; í furstu (1): Olafs. 258, 20; í furstunni
  (1): Olafs. 291, 19–20; (3) *temporal adverbial accusatives :*
  ina níundu hverja nótt (1): Gylf. 76, 13; inn fyrra dag
  (1): Gylf. 76, 19–20; (4) *miscellaneous adverbial phrases :*
  með því (1): Gylf. 10, 14; þaðan af (1): Gylf. 11, 20; af
  ættinni (1): Gylf. 15, 24; af hans heiti (1): Gylf. 27, 5;
  af þessum systkinum (1): Gylf. 37, 18; af nafni hennar
  (1): Gylf. 43, 6; með hánum (1): Gylf. 76, 7; eptir boði
  náttúrunnar (1): Olafs. 104, 6–7; af honum (1): Olafs. 118,
  24; við sinn harm (1): Olafs. 135, 27; með guðs miskun
  ok áeggjan drotníngar (1): Olafs. 141, 22–23; fyrir mar-
  gra luta sakir (1): Olafs. 256, 4; með kappi miklu (1):
  Olafs. 262, 17–18; til lítils (1): Olafs. 285, 2. . . .

C. *Adverbial clause :*
  svá er sagt at þá er hann svaf—Gylf. 9, 6; þetta fór . . . at
  þá er sinarnar knýtti—Eyrb. 88, 15.

D. *Adverb + adverbial phrase :*
þar í eyjunum (1.) : Olafs. 145, 9 ; eigi með nökkuru móti
(1) : Olafs. 266, 20 ; víða um heiminn (1) : 295, 18–19 ;
upp ór hlaðunum (1) : Eyrb. 101, 6.

E. *Adverbial phrase + adverb :*
níu nóttum síðarr (1) : Gylf. 47, 3 ; um morgininn eptir (1) :
Olafs. 128, 16.

F. *Adverbial clause + adverbial phrase :*
at því harðara er þórr knúðiz því fastara (1) : Gylf. 67, 2-3.

G. *Adverbial phrase + adverbial clause + adverb :*
svá at um alt þat ríki, er átt hafði Tryggvi . . . þá : Olafs.
280, 6.

II. *Object, Object + Adverbial Phrase ; Object + Dependent*
Clause.

A. *Object.*
(1) *accusative* of the pronoun : þat (3) : Olafs. 113, 6 ; Gylf.
16, 9 ; 59, 4 ; þetta (4) : Gylf. 26, 21 ; 73, 18 ; 98, 9 ;
Olafs. 118, 5. (2) *nominal accusative :* at öll búsgögn ok
öll reiðigögn (1) : Gylf. 18, 1–2 ; önga frægð (1) : Gylf.
40, 19–20 ; engan knút (1) : Gylf. 59, 17 ; jörðina (1) :
Gylf, 69, 7–8 ; ekki vald (1) : Gylf. 69, 17 ; samflott (1) :
Olafs. 153, 20–21 ; meira (1) : Olafs. 296, 20 and finally
296, 26 : at þenna mann. (3) *pronominal dative :* mér (4) :
Olafs. 102, 2 ; 139, 30 ; Gylf. 210 ; Eyrb. 95, 17–18 ; okkr
(1) : Olafs. 295, 11 ; þér (3) : Gylf. 90, 4-5 ; Eyrb. 16, 17–
18 ; Olafs. 305, 24 ; yðr (2) : Olafs. 286, 8–9 ; Eyrb. 95,
11–12 ; honum or hánum (13) ; Gylf. 37, 7–8 : 56, 1 ; 67,
17 ; 90, 27 ; 90, 29 ; Eyrb. 89, 26 ; 90, 11–12 ; 96, 17,
Olafs. 146, 28 ; 258, 4 ; 268, 18 ; 284, 5 ; 201, 22 ; henni
(1) : Olafs. 103, 3 ; þessu (1) : Gylf. 53, 18–19 ; and finally
þeim (1) : Gylf. 42, 9. (4) *nominal dative :* þessu boði (1) :
Olafs. 279, 28 ; þór ok Óðni (1) : Olafs. 280, 8 ; bóndum
(1) : Olafs. 279, 20 ; þórði (1) : Eyrb. 11, 13 ; hrossum
þorbjarnar (1) : Eyrb. 21, 25–26. (5) *nominal genitive :*
þeirar gjafar (1) : Gylf. 47, 11 ; þess hlutar (1) : Gylf.
56, 8–9.

B. *Object + adverbial phrase :* at bátinn undir honum reiddi
vindr, etc., Olafs. 294, 2.

C. *Object + relative clause:* svá at lutskipti þat alt, er hann fékk i hernaði. . . . Olafs. 258, 1.

D. *Adverbial Accusative + temporal clause:* at annan tíma, er ek kemr. . . . Olafs. 121, 19–20.

III. *Predicate noun,* if placed immediately after the dependent particle, invariably requires inversion :

A. *Predicate Substantive:* svá er sagt, at Arnúlfus hét maðr, Olafs. 105, 29 ; here also belong : Olafs. 116, 4: er Silfraskalli var kallaðr ; 120, 5 : er hinn úngi var kallaðr, and finally Olafs. 142, 22 : er hinn 3 var keisari, the last three showing an emphatic position of the predicate noun in the relative clause.

B. *Predicate Adjective :* sem dauðr sé Knútr, Olafs. 118, 28; at sátt mundi vera þat, Olafs. 254, 14 ; at sundrleit, Olafs. 262, 16 ; er görr var, Gylf. 17, 12 ; at jafnsatt, Gylf. 40, 5 ; þá er full er, Gylf. 80, 17.   Not infrequently the adjective in its attributive form is given the emphatic position, being separated from the subject which it modifies by the predicate : at 2 væri kosti til, Olafs. 126, 17 ; again : Gylf. 49, 10 : at margr kemr sá . . . ; and finally : Olafs. 262, 27 : at allr varð vátr steinninn, in which case the "steinninn" is separated from the modifier "allr" by copula and predicate adjective.

C. *Predicate infinitive :* at dveljaz munu stundirnar, Gylf. 31, 1, and : at eira skyldu eldr ok vatn, Gylf. 73, 11.

D. *Predicate participle :* er átt hafði, Gylf. 32, 9 ; Olafs. 110, 25 ; 117, 20 ; 279, 6 ; 279, 8 ; sem verit höfðu, Olafs. 115, 23 ; at verit hefir, Olafs. 272, 23 ; enn sagt er, Gylf. 31, 1 ; at brotinn var, Gylf. 57, 14 ; ok er búit var, Gylf. 79, 10 ; er brendr er, Gylf. 87, 2-3 ; en fallnir vóru, Eyrb. 86, 28 ; at komit var, Eyrb. 98, 7–8; at rifin var, Eryb. 99, 8 ; while in all the instances just cited the participle is in the past tense, we have in Gylf. 7, 8, a present participle : svát logandi er hann ok brennandi, etc. etc.

B. *Transposed Order.*

Under "Transposition" we understand that arrangement of words in which the subject and the verbal modifiers precede the predicate : *subject + verb-modifiers + verb.* In the partial transposition the predicate may further be followed by verbal modifiers, while the complete transposition does not permit a verbal modifier to follow the predicate. The two possibilities of the transposed order in the case of a simple predicate are thus :

(1) Subject + verbal modifiers + *verb final.*

(2) Subject + verbal modifiers + *verb* + verbal modifiers.

Of the latter type there are exceedingly few instances, so that it may almost be said that if *transposition* of the *simple predicate verb* is used, it is generally in its *complete final form.*

If the predicate is a compound tense of the verb, the arrangement becomes more complicated : it is a question first of the relative position of the constituent parts of the predicate, and secondly of the verbal modifiers. In the case of complete transposition, the auxiliary holds the extreme final position in the sentence, no matter whether it is preceded by verbal modifiers or not : the two possible types being thus :

(1) Subject + verbal noun + *auxiliary final.*

(2) Subject + verbal noun + verb-modifiers + *auxiliary final.*

In the partial transposition of the compound verb the auxiliary must, of course, also follow the verbal noun, while the verb-modifiers are at liberty to follow the auxiliary, thus :

(3) Subject + verbal noun + auxiliary + verb-modifiers.

(4) Subject + verbal noun + verb-modifiers + auxiliary + verb-modifiers.

In the *independent* clause of *Old Norse prose* transposition is almost entirely unknown, and we had to quote the *Poetic Edda* in order to show that it occurs at all in the *Old Norse language.* As regards the dependent clauses, unless prevented by reasons and phenomena requiring inversion, the normal order is by far the predominant mode of dependent expression, there being not a few groups of subordinate clauses without any genuine instance of transposition at all, at least in the 250 pages examined for the purpose. It is on account of the infrequency of the transposed order in Old Norse that no attempt can be made to formulate dogmatic principles and hypotheses as to why transposition is used, and it must suffice to state that it occurs only as an entirely insignificant secondary mode of expressing dependent relation ; with the exception of the adjective clauses in which, as we shall see, it is employed more frequently.

(1) *Substantive clauses.* Neither the *declarative* nor the *imperative sentence* shows a genuine case of transposition. The subject is omitted, although the auxiliary has the final position, in Eyrb. 95, 6 : hón hyggr at eiga mundi ; Eyrb. 96, 1 : ek veit at verða mun ; so also in Gylf. 68, 21–22 . . . ek munda eigi trúa at vera mætti. Once, in Eyrb. 11, 27 : kvað þar engi víg bæta skulu, the subordinate conjunction is omitted and instead of the inversion after "þar" we have transposition. In the *indirect interrogative* clauses, however, there are comparatively more cases of transposed order. Genuine cases are : Gylf. 4, 17 . . . ok spurði hverr höllina átti ; Gylf. 58, 22–23 : þá þóttiz þórr skilja hvat lætum verit hefði of nóttina ; Eyrb. 16, 10 : enn ek kjósa hvárr okkar leysa skal ; further, Eyrb. 22, 28–29 : ok sá hvat er títt var, (observe the "er" after "hvat"), and finally Olafs. 127, 18–19 : ok séam hvat tiltækiligazt þikkir. Transposition of the predicate with the subject omitted and understood is found in : Olafs. 147, 23 : . . . þeir vissu varla . . . hvat vera mundi ; and finally Olafs. 293, 14–15 : vita, hvat valda mundi. Out of 334 normal dependent declarative clauses, 3 are what may be called transposed. Out of 96 normal dependent imperative clauses, 1 is peculiarly transposed. Out of 108 normal dependent interrogative clauses, 5 show genuine, and 2 so-called transposition.

(2) *Adjective clauses.* While in the substantive clauses transposition is of the utmost insignificance, the *dependent relative sentence* shows an entirely different proportion between the normal and transposed arrangements. If out of the 677 clauses, only 485 show normal order, while there are 194 transposed, transposition already begins to play a by no means insignificant rôle. In fact, the dependent relative sentence is perhaps the only one which employs at all the transposed order, if we ignore the 5 cases of the dependent interrogative, because the remaining 4 of the substantive as well as the 32 instances in the adverbial clauses to be discussed later are practically incomplete in their transposition. A more detailed treatment of the adjective clause is, therefore, indispensable. The question why in the relative sentence transposition is so strikingly more frequent than in any other subordinate clause could hardly be answered satisfactorily in a general treatment like this, but would undoubtedly be a subject well worthy of special consideration. I would take the liberty, though, to suggest that such a strange phenomenon *points*, perhaps,

to *an older stage* in *the development of the language*, to a time when transposition had been employed with the same liberty, for instance, as in *Anglo-Saxon* or *Old High German*, and that in a comparatively later process of abandoning such order, it felt especially embarrassed in regard to the relative clause. The *original* parataxis of the *pre-Germanic* relative clause had yielded in the *further development* of the language to the *hypotaxis* as expressed in the *transposed* arrangement. Now, when at a *much later period* the Old Norse abandoned the dependent transposed order without giving up at the same time the dependent hypotactical arrangement, the return to the normal order was especially embarrassing in regard to the relative clause, which had undergone the change from parataxis to transposed hypotaxis and was to receive again the order of the parataxis, that is, the normal order, and the result was that while the new rule broke through in so many instances of the relative clauses, transposition stuck to others of them.

The dependent final verb of the relative clause is separated from its subject by an adverbial expression, an object, and by a predicate noun.

A. *By an adverb:* eptir : Olafs. 105, 14 : þat er eptir var ; aptr, Eyrb. 101, 31 : er aptr géngu ; nærr : Olafs. 282, 28 ; 283, 11 : er nærr var ; inn : Gylf. 38, 12 : er inn gengr inni ; Olafs. 118, 18 ; 119, 1 ; 292, 14: þeir er inni vóru ; hér : Eyrb. 94, 30 : er hér er ; þar : Eyrb. 3, 19 ; 85, 12–13 ; Olafs. 302, 8 : er þar var ; þar til : Gylf. 13, 14 : er þar til liggja ; þá : Olafs. 297, 7 : hverr þá var ; við : Eyrb. 99, 19 : þeir er við vóru ; and finally svá : Olafs. 108, 6 : 142, 20 ; Gylf. 7, 4 ; 15, 5 ; 21, 12 ; 22, 7 ; 30, 7 ; 48, 13 ; 50, 7 and 89, 13 : er svá heita.

B. *Other adverbal expressions (preposition + case)* : í borginni : Olafs. 105, 8 : þat er í borginni var ; með þeim : Olafs. 107, 20 : er með þeim var ; Olafs. 113, 2–3 : er fyrir þeim var ; Olafs. 125, 5 : er á skipinu vóru ; Olafs. 279, 3 ; 303, 11 : er í móti stóð ; Olafs. 282, 11 : er í móti mæla, but immediately after that : ok eigi vilja hlýða. Olafs. 292, 11, 12 : er í skálanum vóru ; Eyrb. 10, 23 : er til skersins lá ; Eyrb. 98, 8 : þeir er í húsinu vóru ; Eyrb. 102, 10 : er við eldinn sátu ; Olafs. 303, 23 : sem í eyjunni var ; Olafs. 304, 23 : er á þau trúa. Gylf. 11, 8 : er ór sárum rann ok laust fór ; Gylf. 15, 16–17 : er eptir henni ferr ; Gylf. 15, 18 : er fyrir henni hleypr ; Gylf. 20, 13 : er til hrímþussa horfir ; Gylf. 22, 17 :

er fyrir ósköpum verða ; Gylf. 28, 1–2 : þeir er í val falla ; Gylf. 48, 12 : er á hans borði stendr ; further in Gylf. 75, 9 : er til þeirar sendiſarar varð ; and finally in the combination of adverb + adverbial phrase : Olafs. 112, 12–13 ; er þar í landi vóru.

A closer observation of all the illustrations cited above will reveal the very interesting fact that with the exception of Olafs. 282, 11 (í móti mæla) and Olafs. 304, 23 (er á þau trúa) in all cases of transposition the final verbs are intransitives : to be (20 times), to become (1) ; to lie (3) ; to go, to run, to ride, to fall (7) ; to sit (1) ; to stand (2) ; while the adverb " svá " is never found in any other connection but with " heita " (10). In other words, out of 46 cases in which an adverb or an adverbial expression precedes the final predicate, 34 all show an intransitive verb, 10 have " heita " preceded by " svá," which almost seems to be a stereotyped phrase, and 2, only, show the variation of preposition plus case + " to speak," and " to believe."

C. *Object*.

> (1) *Pronominal object* precedes the final verb : mér : Eyrb. 95, 24 ; Olafs. 261, 2–3 : sem mér skilja ; honum : Olafs. 131, 6 ; 268, 5 ; 260, 24 : er honum þjónaðu ; henni : Eyrb. 95, 26 : er henni líkar ; hana : Eyrb. 97, 7 ; Gylf. 15, 14 : er hana sœkir ; þeim : Gylf. 8, 3 : sú er þeim fylgði.

> (2) *A substantive object :* Olafs. 136, 11 : er himnum ræðr ok skapat hefir alla luti ; Olafs. 150, 10 : er sigr fengi. Olafs. 281, 19–20 : er alla sér trúliga þjónandi elskar ok auðgar. Olafs. 284, 17, 18 : er Ísland byggvir. Eyrb. 85, 25 : er vápnin sóttu. Olafs. 295, 20 : er þann sið hafa ; Gylf. 12, 14 : er heim byggja ; Gylf. 53, 19–20 : sá er flestu illu ræðr ; Gylf. 70, 8 : þá er mikinn mátt hafa, and finally Eyrbyggja 92, 6 : er þrælana átti ; altogether 19 cases.

An attempt to *classify the final verbs* preceded by an object is more difficult, there being no such definite lines as in the case of adverbs and adverbial expressions. The auxiliary " to have " (to get, to be in possession of) occurs 4 times ; " to seem, to deem, to please, to love " 6 cases ; " to be at the head " 2 cases ; " to obey, to serve " (2), " to inhabit " (2) ; " to seek " (2) and " to see " (1).

D. *Predicate noun* is more frequently found before the final verb than all the above-mentioned groups counted together. It occurs :

(1) As a *substantive* 89 times, the majority of which, 58, is found in the Prose Edda, as : 7, 3 ; 7, 7 ; 13, 9 ; 14, 2 ; 14, 4 ; 14, 5 ; 14, 19 ; 15, 6 ; 15, 22 ; 18, 1 ; 24, 5 ; 24, 14-15 ; 25, 2 ; 25, 4 ; 25, 6 ; 25, 11 ; 26, 11, 12 ; 27, 4 ; 27, 18 ; 30, 2-3 ; 32, 6 ; 32, 7-8 ; 33, 9-10 ; 34, 10 ; 35, 21 ; 37, 9 ; 39, 19 ; 40, 13 ; 41, 10 ; 41, 12 ; 42, 5-6 ; 42, 14-15 ; 43, 1 ; 43, 6 ; 45, 9 ; 47, 10-11 ; 48, 5-6 ; 49, 13-14 ; 49, 15, etc. on almost every page. Olafs. 103, 4 ; 106, 15 ; 106, 22 ; 107, 3 ; 107, 21 ; 108, 20 ; 108, 24 ; 109, 26 ; 114, 28 ; 115, 25 ; 139, 3 ; 145, 5 ; 153, 4 ; 153, 14-15 ; 154, 28 ; 250, 21 ; 260, 1 ; 265, 7 ; Eyrb. 3, 7 ; 3, 8 ; 4, 27 ; 4, 28 ; 8, 27 ; 8, 29 ; 13, 10 ; 13, 10 ; 18, 6 ; 21, 16 ; 21, 23 ; 92, 24 ; 96, 28. Almost in each of these instances we find the formula : sá er + Proper name + heitir, or hét, or heita, or hétu. Of other cases : Gylf. 81, 11 : þá verðr þat er mikil tíðindi þykkja ; Gylf. 43, 1 : henni þjóna þær er meyjar andaz ; in Eyrb. 96, 28 the predicate substantive is a preposition + proper noun : . . . þeir kómust á bæ þann, er "í Nesi" heitir "hinu neðra" (observe the peculiar position of neðra).

(2) *As* an *adjective* 16 times : Olafs. 105, 9 : þat er fémætt var ; Olafs. 117, 13 : Norðimbraland, er heiðit var ; Olafs. 256, 25 : þat er meira var ; Eyrb. 85, 3 : vápn þau er þýngst vóru ; Eyrb. 92, 29 : þann er afbragðligr væri ; Eyrb. 94, 23 : þat er flatt lá. Eyrb. 97, 19 : klæði þau, er vát vóru ; and finally in Gylf. 9, 16 : er saltir váru ; 11, 8 : er . . . laust fór ; 11, 15 : er lausir fóru ; 27, 3 : er skylt er 27, 5 : er blítt er ; 34, 15 : er vitrastr er ; 43, 6-7 : er fagrt er ; 44, 12-13 : sá er hóflátr er ; 62, 13 : sá er síðarst gekk.

Reviewing the transposition in the relative clause, it will be found that out of 194 cases in the 170 instances quoted above the dependent predicate was a simple verb. Thus only 24 cases are left in which the dependent predicate is a compound tense of the verb : Olafs. 110, 29 : þess, er sagt er : 150, 15 : er berjast skyldu ; 258, 12 : er látit höfðu ; 258, 14 : er átt höfðu ; in Eyrb. 9, 8 : er hafa vildi ; 22, 29 : þat er mælt er ; 102, 3 : er látizt höfðu ; in Gylf. 6, 14 : er lifa skal ok aldri týnaz ; 6, 7 : er brotin váru ; 22, 4 : er fara vilja ; 22, 9-10 : er borít verðr ; 99, 2 : er kaupa vildi ; 100, 19-20 : er yrkja kunnu, and in the five instances of Olafs. 302, 9-10, in which the auxiliary is also a compound tense : . . .

er Hákon jarl hafði gera látit,"—in all these instances, 14 in number, the auxiliary immediately follows the verbal noun, being separated by no verbal modifier and occupying the extreme end position.   In other cases, however, (10) : Olafs. 136, 12 : er . . . skapat hefir alla luti ; Eyrb. 11, 27: þau er orðit höfðu á þórsnesi ; in Gylf. 15, 25 : er kallaðr er Mánagarmr, so further: 24, 14 ; 29, 15 ; 61, 5 ; 63, 9 ; 81, 4 : er kallaðr er fimbulvetr ; further in 45, 4 : er þjóna skulu í Valhöll, and finally in 83,20 : er bundinn er fyrir Gnípahelli,—the auxiliary also follows immediately after the verbal noun, but precedes some modifier of the dependent verb. Among the relative clauses no instance was found showing the type : Subject + verbal noun + verb-modifier + auxiliary plus or minus verbal modifier, a type which is, in fact, rare in any dependent clause.

(3) *Adverbial clauses.*   Hardly two genuine instances of complete transposition are found among the different adverbial clauses. All the illustrations to be mentioned under this heading are incomplete.   In most of them the subject is understood and omitted. We can speak only of a more or less close approach to transposition :

A. *Local clause :* Gylf. 55, 8 : hvert er—wherever—fara skal (Subject omitted).

B. *Temporal clause :* Gylf. 57, 2 : en er soðit var ; Eyrb. 11, 8 : meðan barizt var ; Eyrb. 102, 14 : meðan sætt er ; and, finally, the only good instance in Olafs. 129, 23–24 : er konúngr hafði skírast látit = "als der König sich hatte taufen lassen."

C. *Modal-Manner clause.*   The phrase : "svá sem sagt er " in : Gylf. 49, 4 ; 77, 13 ; or "svá sem hér segir" in : Gylf. 10, 17 ; 12, 10 ; 24, 6 ; 26, 13 ; 31, 13 ; "sem fyrr segir": Eyrb. 7, 12 : Other incomplete cases are Gylf. 65, 11 : enn mér líz ; 66, 10 : sem mik varði ; 69, 6–7 ; sem þér sýndiz ; 70, 1–2 : sem síðar varð ; Eyrb. 22, 25–26 : sem yðr líkar ; 104, 10 : sem komit var ; Olafs. 256, 20 : enn réttligt var ; 305, 6–7 : sem hverjum sýnist.

D. *Causal.*   The only and at the same time incomplete case : Olafs. 291, 7 : þvíat mér leiðist.

E. *Final* clause. Eyrb. 95, 23–24 : . . . til þess, at henni líki." Incomplete and only case.

F. *Consecutive-Result clause.*   The only 2 cases : Olafs. 282, 26–27 : svá at skilja mætti ; and Gylf. 97, 17 . . . svá at spyrja kunni hann fróðleiks, are incomplete.

G. *Conditional clause.* Olafs. 261, 5 : enn ef svá er, and Olafs. 296, 16 : ef yðr þikkir, are again no genuine cases. Peculiar is : Olafs. 295, 25 : ef hann vill kristinn gerast, which is neither normal nor transposed.

VITA.

The author was born the 4th of May, 1870, in Mitau, Kurland, Russia. Having received his preliminary education in private schools and by private tutors, he entered the Classical Gymnasium in Mitau, the former "Gymnasium Academicum," in January, 1882. December 19, 1890, he received from the same institution the "testimonium maturitatis," having passed the series of examinations known as the "Abiturienten examen," which latter involved—according to the regulations of said institution—an eight-years' course of study in the German, Russian and Latin languages and literatures, in mathematical and historical branches, and a six-years' course in the Greek language and literature. In February, 1893, he entered the School of Philosophy of Columbia University, received the degree of M.A. in June, 1894, and studied till May, 1895. He took the following courses : Arabic and Hebrew, under Prof. R. J. H. Gottheil ; the German, Old Norse, and Scandinavian literatures, and "Faust," under the late Prof. H. H. Boyesen ; Germanic philology, Old High German, and Icelandic, under Prof. W. H. Carpenter ; Gothic and Middle High German, under Mr. E. H. Babbitt ; Anglo-Saxon language and Historical English (Early and Middle English), Anglo-Saxon poetry, Linguistics, and Zoroaster's teaching, under Prof. A. V. W. Jackson ; Anglo-Saxon Syntax and Chaucer, under Prof. Th. R. Price. Further : History of French literature in the 18th century (Voltaire), under Prof. A. Cohn ; and, finally, Philosophy of Kant and his successors—Fichte, Schelling, Hegel, etc., under Prof. N. M. Butler.

He is at present engaged as Instructor of English to foreigners in Evening School No. 27 (under Dr. J. S. Taylor), and as Instructor of German in Grammar Schools No. 2 (under Dr. W. L. Ettinger), No. 12 (under Mr. J. F. Townley), No. 96 (under Mr. B. W. Purcell), and No. 18 (under Dr. B. C. Magie).

He wishes to express his heartiest thanks to Prof. W. H. Carpenter for the painstaking correction of the proof sheets of the present thesis, a correction which required much time and energy.

www.ingramcontent.com/pod-product-compliance
Lightning Source LLC
Chambersburg PA
CBHW032346020726
47499CB00009B/3185